Niall Hemingway is an actor and writer. They live in London with their husband and dog. They have been writing for the last few years, focusing on stories that champion LGBTQIA+ characters. They believe the backdrop of folklore and myth is the perfect world to get lost in.

For my husband Stewart Hemingway

And the first believer, Kate Chubb

Niall Hemingway

THE SON OF CIRCE

Vol. 1

AUSTIN MACAULEY PUBLISHERS
LONDON · CAMBRIDGE · NEW YORK · SHARJAH

Copyright © Niall Hemingway 2024

The right of Niall Hemingway to be identified as author of this work has been asserted by the author in accordance with sections 77 and 78 of the Copyright, Designs and Patents Act 1988.

All rights reserved. No part of this publication may be reproduced, stored in a retrieval system, or transmitted in any form or by any means, electronic, mechanical, photocopying, recording, or otherwise, without the prior permission of the publishers.

Any person who commits any unauthorised act in relation to this publication may be liable to criminal prosecution and civil claims for damages.

This is a work of fiction. Names, characters, businesses, places, events, locales, and incidents are either the products of the author's imagination or used in a fictitious manner. Any resemblance to actual persons, living or dead, or actual events is purely coincidental.

A CIP catalogue record for this title is available from the British Library.

ISBN 9781035849314 (Paperback)
ISBN 9781035849321 (Hardback)
ISBN 9781035849338 (ePub e-book)

www.austinmacauley.com

First Published 2024
Austin Macauley Publishers Ltd®
1 Canada Square
Canary Wharf
London
E14 5AA

1

The island of Aeaea stood cloaked in the Ionian Sea. It could not be plotted on any map, and those that tried found the markings on their papers would not hold. It was cloaked in a deep magic that was wrought by the witch of Aeaea, Circe. She was tall, with burnt copper hair that looked as though it were on fire when the sun hit. It often sat in a messy but practical bun. Her eyes were deep hazelnut pools etched with wisdom and a fierceness that some said came from her father, Helios, the Titan Sun God. In reality, it came from the history of her suffering and torment before Aeaea. She was a woman of wild beauty who most mortals found enticing and terrifying in equal measure.

Most who stumbled upon her island never left the beach of white sand and never stayed longer than the passing of a night. But there were some men who were curious and greedy to explore. These men rarely left Aeaea again. The island had been cultivated by Circe. She knew every plant, tree, and animal that moved on its land. As she cared for them, in return they cared for her. If any living thing was harmed or taken, she would know, for her magic connected her to everything.

So, when those men left the beach to hunt in her forests, she would hunt them. When she found her prey, Circe would transform them into beasts, guiding them back to the beach where they would be trapped, killed, and eaten by those of their crew that had stayed behind. Every now and again, a man would make it through the forest and find the home of the fearsome witch. This meant he had not harmed any living creature, eaten any of the forest fruits, nor picked any of the plants or herbs. He would be welcomed by the witch. She would share food with him and invite the man to her bed, and so that's how things were for centuries.

The day that began the change of all things was one like any other. Autumn had fallen on the island in cool winds that whipped the leaves of the trees, and the sun had faded into a pale yellow that lit the late afternoon sky. Circe stared up and thought momentarily of her father, Helios. That, in itself, should have told her today would be different as she hadn't thought about him for an age. Pulling up the last of her herbs, Circe meandered her way up to her altar that sat at the highest point of Aeaea.

Her altar was a simple stone table adorned with a pestle and mortar, a copper bowl, a knife made of bone, and some beeswax candles. The start of the stream that cut through the woodlands until it reached the sea was on the left. Circe bent down to fill an ornate goblet with its fresh water before placing it upon the alter. A great boar was snuffling in the grass nearby.

"Do you mind? I need quiet," she chided the hairy beast. It huffed in response and lay itself down by the stream, its snout touching the fresh cool water. Circe smiled and nodded her thanks before turning to begin her ritual. She began to crush the herbs, letting the sweet smell rise to fill her nose. She sighed in contentedness at the familiarity of this magic.

Next, she picked up a candle and blew on the wick, which sparked its flame. A grin spread over her face; she loved spell casting, and this particular spell brought with it a sense of pride. This spell kept the gods themselves at bay. Circe never cared for the Olympians. They were meddlesome, always pulling others into the trials of their heroes. Her magic, too, inspired a great deal of envy, jealousy, and, in her mind fear. It is best they be kept away. However, there are some things that even magic cannot keep at bay.

It was a small change—a change that, to any mortal, would go unnoticed. As Circe picked up her bone knife, like she had a thousand times before, she felt it. The boar by the stream had felt it too. It moved to put itself between Circe and this unexpected intruder. Circe raised her hand above her head, moving it as though through water. She then knelt to push her palms into the earth, confirming her suspicion. Time had stopped.

All things had stopped growing and breathing except herself and the boar, perhaps because they were inside the power of the altar. "Stay close to me, my friend," she whispered to the beast. Standing with her back to the altar, the bone knife still in hand, her strong, deep voice rang out, "Reveal yourself to me. I fear you not."

Shimmering into place before the witch were three women. Almost identical in appearance, wearing robes of light grey delicately embroidered with fine gold, each had jet black hair that fell in a braid to the waist. They all had the same colour in their eyes, that of a clouded ocean green. Circe looked closer at the intruders; she noticed the one on the left was the younger of the three and the one on the right was the oldest. The streaks of grey in her hair gave her away. The middle woman held in her hand an orb that swirled with the same ocean green colour in their eyes. Now she knew who had invaded her island; there was no mistaking.

"Klotho, Lakhesis, and Atropos. To what do I owe the honour of the Fates on my island?" Circe asked in a calm, cool manner.

Klotho answered, her voice sweet and tempered, "Circe, great witch of Aeaea, we sisters never show ourselves to anyone without permission of the gods."

"Today is the day we must." Lakhesis came in next with a voice that was motherly, but it had a sharpness to it that made Circe feel as though she was in trouble.

"We have seen this day coming since the dawn of time, before even the first mortal thread had been woven." Atropos spoke now, a voice of assertiveness and wisdom. "Destiny is fixed as we decide, but today, Circe, great witch, you too must decide."

"Me?" It caught her so off guard, as this was not the way of the Fates. It had always been they who weaved the thread, fixing destinies, and cutting life short at the time they decided. Circe stared at each of the Fates, her mind whirling, trying to decipher what they were up to. "What trick is this? What game do you play? I will be no part of the games between gods and men."

"The Olympians have no knowledge of our being here," Klotho spoke in a hushed voice, as though anyone might overhear.

"You need not whisper, sister; we are outside of time, and the magic of this island has us cloaked, am I correct?" asked Lakhesis.

"You are." Circe replied, making no attempt to hide the pride in her voice, "Though I was just reaffirming the spell when you arrived."

"We know, but our meeting had to be now. You alone have a choice to make, a choice that will shape the future of Greece and, indeed, the world." Atropos said with a grounded urgency. As she spoke, she pulled at one of the golden threads on her robe and stretched it between her sisters; Klotho held one and Atropos the other. "This is your thread, Circe. Wound into it are the threads of potential life. Three sons have already been," Atropos pointed to three knots, "but there is another."

"Another?" asked Circe.

"Yes. Life is waiting to be born." Klotho smiled. "Three you have already been given by the wily Odysseus, but there is the potential and need of another. That is why we have come."

Circe felt her head swimming with the information that was being imparted to her.

Lakhesis tilted her head to one side, watching all the expressions on Circe's face. "The fourth child is our concern. Their existence is entirely your choice… out of our control, something that has never happened. For we know when all beings will be born, but this fourth child…"

"How is it that you cannot tell me more about this other?" asked Circe.

"It's unclear. There are things that have been set in time that must and will be… Others come and go. There is a war that will come between the gods; it is fixed and will be, but the outcome… is uncertain. Uncertain because of you." Atropos pointed a long, thin finger towards Circe. "All we can see is this… If this fourth child is born, it will change the outcome of the War of Olympus."

"Now I see… You have come to me to save the gods?" Circe smirked.

"It is not so simple. The outcome of the Olympian War will shape the future of all of the world. If this child is never born, then Olympus and the mortal world will fall and cease to be. If the child is born… the future is still uncertain… but there is a future for the mortals and perhaps some kind of hope for the Olympians," Klotho pleaded.

"If this child is so important, why is it not fixed as my other sons were?"

"We think it is because of you. Your magic. The father of this child must have divine blood; the spell that keeps them at bay must be keeping the child at bay." Lakhesis scolded, "Herein lies your choice!"

"It is not simple for you we know." Atropos said, seeing the resignation on Circe's face. "The gods have maligned you, and that has scarred you, but this child… this child is needed for us all. We must leave before our absence is noted; we have risked much by coming to you." Atropos pressed her end of Circe's thread to her robe, and it disappeared back into the embroidery. As quickly as they arrived, they had gone, leaving Circe and the boar alone again atop the mountain. The wind brushed against her cheek, gently informing her time had resumed again. She looked into the big pig's eyes and exhaled a long breath.

2

Circe stood motionless, faintly aware of the coolness of the bone knife still gripped tightly in her hand.

"What am I to do with this knowledge?" Her words fell into the wind. She wanted nothing to do with gods, let alone bed one. The thought of sleeping with an Olympian made her blood run cold. She wouldn't do it. There, that's that.

She had decided that the spell would be cast again. Her hand moved to pick up the beeswax candle as she had before the interruption, brought it to her mouth to blow it into life, but then she stopped.

"Can I deny this life being born?" The boar turned its head to the side in answer.

"I don't know how it might affect the future, only that it will. Who would be its father? Can I choose that? It is too much."

Circe stalked away from the alter, back down toward her home, the brown boar following along after. All the way, she didn't stop working through the possibilities, muttering aloud and attracting the attention of other animals on the island, each offering a call in response to her various questions.

As Circe stepped over the threshold of her home, she turned to face the gathered horde of beasts and said, "Be not offended, but tonight I will sleep alone," With that she closed the rough-cut wooden door.

Sleep would have been welcomed this night, but it seemed to evade Circe, completely driven away by the volume of her thoughts. A child who has a destiny beyond that of anyone who has lived before, but she too had a choice to allow the child to be. It would be simple, she thought, if the war of Olympus meant the end of the Olympians, and that was all. There was no love lost between Circe and the gods.

When she was a young woman still living in the house of her father, Helios, deemed her to be the runt of his children. Mocked openly at feasts, Ares once called her a serving whore and would not allow her at the table. Helios found this so entertaining that he nicknamed her *"Porni,"* forcing her to wait on the God of War's every need. When he vowed to take her to bed, even then, Helios did not object, telling her plainly, "If you, my little *Porni*, can fight off the God of War, then he will not bed you," his cold laugh still echoed in her memories.

She of course knew she could not fight off Ares, so she went to him only to be faced with more of his cruelty, as loudly before the gathered gods and Nymphs he declared, "You really thought that I, Ares, would bed a beast like you? Helios, how do you bear this child of yours?" His voice was harsh, like a whip.

"I don't." Helios roared with laughter.

She thought then how cold her father's laugh sounded when he was the God of the Sun. The final break for her and the gods came the night she was banished to Aeaea. She had become quite adept with her magic by now and had transformed a nymph called Scylla into a many-headed tentacled beast, a hideous monster that was doomed to lurk in a narrow passage of the ocean to devour sailors. This type of transformation enraged the gods, as they were the only ones meant to be able to curse with transformation. Their rage grew when they found that they were unable to undo Circe's magic; even the great Zeus was unable to undo what had been done. As punishment, Zeus decreed that Helios must banish Circe, for she had offended the order of power, and deep down she knew she had made them afraid.

"Circe, you have brought shame on me since the moment you were born, and now you extend that shame further to the Olympians. You are banished from the halls and places of the Olympians and Titans. Banished to the wild island of Aeaea, where you will be lost and forgotten."

With a wave of his hand, Circe felt the ground below begin to burn the soles of her feet. She turned and ran until she made it out of the Hall of Helios. Circe didn't stop running until she reached the stream that ran by the base of the mountain. A sea nymph was waiting by the bank of a stream and, in a soft voice, said, "Circe, outcast, I am sent to see you arrive at Aeaea." She reached out her hand.

Circe took it as they stepped into the river. All waters connect; it is how nymphs travel. Though Circe had done it before with her mother, this time it felt colder, and the salt burnt her skin as they passed through the ocean tides. Then, in no time at all, they were stepping on to cool white sand. Circe turned to thank the nymph only, to see she had already gone.

Alone. For the first time in her life.

Circe had thought it might have been terrifying to be so alone, but instead, a deep sense of peace flooded her. It was a peace that she refused to ever surrender. Over centuries, as her power grew, the island and the witch became one. As is custom, power always draws the attention of gods, so they began showing up to torment and mock her. That is all except Artemis, Goddess of the Hunt.

Artemis had rich brown hair that was plaited and wrapped up into a bun. A silver crown with a crescent moon of opal adorned her head, and at her back was a bow made of antler. She was draped in a robe of woodland green tied at the waist with a brown rope, her feet were bare, and she made no sound as she walked. Her most striking feature were her eyes—a fierce yellow like those of an eagle. Artemis had kept her eye on Circe from the moment of birth, drawn to the wildness in her that she so loved.

She had watched as Circe tamed the wild Aeaea, admiring the respect she offered all living things in life and in death. On a night when the moon was full, Artemis landed on the witch's island and silently moved through the forest, making her way to the house of Circe. As she reached the clearing before the grey stone building, Circe stepped out to greet her.

"Yet another Olympian darkens my island!" Circe remarked coolly, "Is it not enough you cast me out? You all must take turns to come and torment me still?"

Artemis fixed her eyes on Circe, and in an honest, heartfelt voice, she replied, "You have indeed been cruelly treated by my kin". The two women watched each other for a moment, Circe letting the words sink in. "I come to ask your permission to rest on your island for a short time."

"Why?" Circe took a step forward, wary of the politeness that faced her. "Why do you, Artemis, seek my permission? None have before! Is this the beginning of some wicked joke?"

Artemis stood still. The hunter in her knew the signs of a creature who felt threatened, and that made them dangerous. She raised her hands to show she meant no harm.

"I do not joke. I have watched you since birth, drawn to your wild spirit. I have seen you tame and cultivate this place, showing respect for all things living, even in death. If you were not already blessed, I would have taken you as a hunter of Artemis. I wish to rest here a time away from Olympus; you are not the only being that is prey to their games." A bitterness stung the last few words she spoke, it was a bitterness Circe knew well.

"You may rest on my island, but you are forbidden to hunt here."

It was bold to command a god, but Circe had never forgotten the fear that led to her exile. "You must always announce your arrival and never bring anyone else here."

Artemis smiled, "I swear it."

"Then you are welcome," Circe turned on her heels and went back inside, leaving the door open, through which Artemis followed her.

Over time, a span of one hundred years or so, the two great women forged a friendship. Artemis honoured the terms set out by Circe, announcing her arrival in the form of a large buzzard hawk that arrived the morning of the night she would arrive. Circe and Artemis moved with respect; a respect that grew deeper when the God of the Hunt would share stories of her own misfortune at the hands of her fellow gods. Mocking her about her wanting to stay chaste, for preferring to be in the forest than on Olympus, and for spurning various affections of other gods. It gave Circe great comfort to know that even a goddess as powerful as Artemis could fall foul of other immortals. It felt odd to trust an Olympian, and yet she did.

It had been nearly a year since Artemis had last set down on Aeaea. Circe found herself searching the sky for any sign of the buzzard hawk; she had missed the company to which she had become accustomed. Picking up a small basket, Circe glided out the front door and over the clearing into the forest to gather herbs and plants for a spell that had come to her in her dreams. Though she did not know its purpose, she felt its power in her core as she always did. As she was picking some lavender, the hair on the back of her arms prickled; something was amiss.

"Lend me your eyes, sweet falcon." Her eyes changed from their deep hazelnut to those of a flacon flying overhead. The bird flew in a slow circle, its eyes bearing down, scouring every inch of the island until they saw it.

Just like that, Circe's eyes were her own again, and she set off at a pace towards the intruder. As she ran, a swarm of animals came to her side: boars, lynx, and mountain lions. As they breached the edge of the forest and into the clearing before her home, she pulled the bone knife from her waist and held it tight in her grip as she planted her feet into the earth, her beast horde grunting and huffing behind her.

"You have broken our agreement! After all this time, you have betrayed me, Artemis." A crackle of pain echoed in her voice.

"Circe, I did not have time to send my winged herald," Artemis answered as she moved to stand in front of something.

"That is the least of your broken vows." Circe gestured with her knife for Artemis to step aside. She did it slowly.

"You *dare* to bring a mortal here? Of all these things, to bring another being to *my* island." The knife she held pointed directly at the young mortal that stood before her.

"I told you plainly… I have shared my secrets with you, and still… still you did this."

Artemis moved towards Circe, only to have her way blocked by a group of boars that set themselves between her and the witch.

"Understand me, Circe; I had no choice and little time to think. Lower your knife and hear me speak please," Circe did not lower her knife.

"This is Kallisto, my handmaiden; Zeus has set his sights on her. He has violated her once before, and she gave him a child; now he wants more of her. I will not let him have her, she is mine! The attention also brings the wrath of Hera, whom I have narrowly saved her from already. I need to hide her from them, and I thought I could do that here with you."

"You would risk bringing Zeus and his wife to my home? After everything I have shared with you… How dare you!"

"Watch your tone, Circe. I am still a god!" Artemis roared in retort.

"And there it is! That Olympian arrogance, but you forget to whom you speak!" Circe sheathed her knife and grabbed a pouch tied to her waist. "Sleep", she whispered, and tipped the contents into the air. Within a moment, Artemis fell to the floor in a deep sleep. Then she turned her attention to Kallisto, a small, light-haired young woman with fierce blue eyes.

"Please," Kallisto pleaded as she dropped to her knees. "Please, great Circe, do not punish me. I did not seek to be brought here; I desire nothing more than to leave. Have mercy, please."

Circe knelt down and lifted the girl by the chin to look her in the eyes. "I know it is no fault of yours. You are a pawn in a game of gods. Stand please."

Circe helped Kallisto to her feet and offered her a warm smile. "I will not harm you. Tell me, what is it you want?"

Kallisto thought for a moment before saying, "Truthfully," she glanced over at Artemis sleeping, then back to Circe, "I want to be free of gods. I know I shouldn't say it, and I am grateful for all I have learnt under Artemis, but I don't want to be a plaything to them. I am no toy to pick up and use when they want."

Circe considered the young woman before her.

"I can hide you from them for as long as you live." She nodded and moved into her house, waving for the girl to follow. Stepping into her kitchen, she started to grind herbs, and as she did so, she asked Kallisto to light a fire and place a small black pot over the flames. Circe moved like water as she muttered words and picked up different plants to cut and press. The witch plucked some fur from a bowl on a shelf and then pulled a strand of hair from Kallisto's head. Holding a bowl of water to her lips, she asked her to spit into it. Kallisto did. The bowl of spittle and water were poured into the black pot as Circe began chanting, adding in the various vegetation in exact amounts at the perfect moment. Magic to Circe was like breathing. There was a smell filling the house now —one of fresh woodland mixed with something damp and furry. Circe removed the pot from the flame, decanted it into a small bottle, and stoppered it before asking Kallisto to follow her back outside.

"I will ask you one last time: is this what you truly desire?" Circe's voice was calm, motherly.

Kallisto nodded.

"Very well. Take this vial tonight when the moon is full and at its highest point. Drink it down and run. It will transform you into a great bear, and that will keep you hidden until your dying breaths. Do you understand?"

"I do," Kallisto answered as she took the vial from Circe's hand. "What of Artemis?"

"It is time she woke up; don't you think?" Circe waved a hand over the sleeping goddess, and she began to stir. Within seconds, Artemis was on her feet, her eyes ablaze with fury. Her bow was drawn, aimed at Circe's throat.

"HOW DARE YOU! I AM A DAUGHTER OF ZEUS!" she roared.

"I know who you are." She replied calmly, pushing the bow and arrow down. "I have done what you have asked; Kallisto will be safe."

"You have?" Artemis softened, "My Kallisto is safe?"

"You may take her back to the mainland, knowing she is protected from all that may cause her harm." Circe kept her voice level and her eyes fixed on Artemis.

"Come, my Kalli." The goddess offered her hand to Kallisto, who took it gently. "Thank you, Circe."

"It is done. Now go, before all Olympus finds its eyes here…" Circe was alone once more, and finally, the spell she had dreamt of the night before suddenly made sense. She turned on her heels and went to find the basket she had dropped. It was time to keep the gods off of her island and away from her forever. Or so she had thought.

It had been so long since she had thought of Artemis and Kallisto. She had felt used and betrayed by the only god she had considered a friend. As the light of the fresh morning sun crept in through the windows, the whirring of her mind finally became still. She knew what she was going to do.

Have the child.

However, she had worked out her own rules; after all, if the child was free of fate, then so was she in deciding how they would come to be. If the child must have Olympian blood, then it would be with the god of her choosing, but Circe, the witch of Aeaea, would not let herself be violated. No, she could concoct a potion or spell that could allow her to conceive. All she needed was a gods essence.

3

The wards had been down on the island for a few days, but no god or goddess had bothered Circe as she toiled with her herbs. Chopping this, muddling that, smelling, tasting, discarding, and starting all over again. All the while muttering combinations of words, jotting down those that felt right, and groaning at those that didn't. It was close, her potion, she could feel it, all that was needed was the ichor of divinity and something she couldn't put her finger on. That was the nature of these things; real magic comes only to fruition at the right moment. She knew in her soul to trust that the last ingredient would show itself when it was time. The spell, however, came in bursts. Every time she found the right ingredient to the potion, so too came the words, fast and deliberate, on her tongue. Her eyes drifted out the window of the witch's kitchen; the moon was at its fullest, hanging bright and pale in the sky.

"The time has come, old friend," she whispered as she wiped her hands on a piece of tattered cloth and moved outside into the clearing.

The island was deathly quiet, as though every living thing was holding its breath. Circe swallowed any feeling of anxiety or fear and pulled herself to her fullest height, raised her arms to the sky, and called out in a strong commanding voice.

"Artemis, Goddess of the Hunt, I call you to me, my old friend. Find your way to Aeaea and be welcomed". She stood as still as stone, waiting to see if Artemis would indeed come. The sound of feathered wings whispered through the air. Circe smiled and said, "Hello old friend".

"Friend? Is that what you call us?" Artemis was cool and bitter. "You deny my return to your island, and you took my Kallisto from me. Now you summon me here as a *friend?*" She let out a dry laugh.

"Time heals all wounds. I forgive you for breaking your oath…"

"I don't forgive you! Your witchery took my Kallisto from me, and then you kept me at bay to cower away from me…" Artemis spat in retort.

"I did only what Kallisto asked of me—to be free of the gods. Before you interrupt me again, I implore you to hear me." Circe paused until Artemis nodded her consent for her to continue. "Thank you. I can help you find Kallisto again but know there is no way to undo my spell if she does not wish it, for my magic is a work of will, mine, and for whom the spell is for. I admit I was rash, angry and not in my coolest head with what happened those years passed, for that, I offer my apologies," Circe spoke honestly, calmly letting the weight of her words reach beneath the stubborn heart of the goddess before her.

Artemis stood regal and silent, watching Circe as a predator does its prey, searching every inch of her for a hint of deception. She could not see it, so she replied with a warmth that spoke of their friendship past, "I too am sorry for breaking my oath, I had wanted to return to you often to scold you but also to make it up to you. Circe know my betrayal was never malicious. If there had been another way…"

"All is in the past." Circe stepped to her friend and placed a hand on her arm, "I will help you find Kallisto… If you can help me with something."

"Whatever you need."

Circe led Artemis inside and shared everything, deciding that complete honesty would be crucial to gaining the trust and aid she needed. She spoke of the war between the Olympians, the child free of fate, and how she needed the blood of a god to secure the divinity of the child to be.

"You ask a lot of me," Artemis responded after a time. "You are sure that without the child, Olympus and the world will fall?"

"I trust the Fates." Circe stood, pacing the room. "I know I ask a lot, but it is the only way I can bring this child forth. I would ask for your aid in trapping a god here… just long enough for me to get what I need."

Artemis felt an uneasiness ripple through her at the memory of Circe's power and how she had so easily put her to sleep. "Who? Have you thought that far ahead?"

"I have had ideas… Hermes? Ares?"

"Ares? Ha! Now that would be revenge, but his divinity is too primal and base, you need another. Apollo."

"Your brother?" Circe hadn't even entertained the thought, she thought it would be cruel to ask Artemis to trick her twin.

"My brother," she answered softly, deep in thought. "What if you do not need to take the blood by deception? What if it is freely given?"

It was as though Circe had been struck by lightning, everything fell into place. "Blood freely given... Do you think he would?"

"Give me the rest of this night to speak with him. I know you are wary, Circe, but you must trust me." She rested her hand affectionately on Circe's cheek. Circe gave a slight nod in acceptance, and as quickly as Artemis had appeared, she had gone.

Now all there was to do was wait. Wait, and of course, finish the incantation. She meditated on the words she had and felt the last few tantalisingly close on her tongue; they just couldn't seem to find their rhythm. As was her custom with magic, she never dwelt too long, for spells never work right when they are forced, so with a sigh of resignation, she decided to take a walk. Circe drifted aimlessly through the woods. The moonlight fell through the leaves overhead and speckled the forest floor with flecks of white. It was in this moment that Circe realised how much she truly had missed the company of Artemis, and for the first time, since her sons with Odysseus had left and passed on, Circe acknowledged her feelings of loneliness.

As she crested the highest point of the island, she could see the pale pink light of dawn creeping up over the horizon.

"My Eos, you look beautiful this morning". Circe sat by her altar and watched the sun grow ever higher, the night had passed, and Artemis had not yet returned. The old feelings of betrayal and doubt bubbled in Circe's stomach. Had she really told Artemis everything and expected any different? Perhaps she thought Circe was lying and up to something cruel, so she went to warn Zeus. Circe looked to the sky, daring a thunderbolt to strike her dead at any moment. The moment didn't come. Pulling herself up to her feet, she was about to start her way back to her house when a soft warmth grazed the back of her neck and a familiar sound of feathered wings tickled her ear. She turned around to face, on the other side of her stone altar, Artemis, and her twin brother Apollo.

The sight of Apollo caught Circe's breath. He stood barechested with a wrap of white and gold around his waist. The definition of every muscle on his body caught the light in the most perfect way to highlight its tone and strength. His eyes held the same yellow as his sister, though in truth they were more golden and held a hypnotising warmth. The rich golden hair atop his head fell to his shoulders and was tied back. He really was striking to behold, and Circe could see why men and women both desired him.

"Welcome, fair Apollo, to my island." Circe greeted him coolly.

"It is a pleasure to finally meet the great witch, Circe." Apollo answered with warmth and musicality, "I have heard much of you and your magic. You struck a certain unease amongst my family, especially when you held us from your island. Did you know even Zeus couldn't break through your spell?"

Circe couldn't help but smile, "I didn't."

"Quite the scandal, actually. Still, that's the past, you needn't worry about prying eyes now, I think they have forgotten all about you, and probably think you are long since dead." There was no malice in his voice, but still, it stung at Circe's pride. "I have listened to all Artemis had to say and consulted my own divinations. The war indeed looms, although I can't see its cause or outcome, so I come to willingly gift my blood to you that you might make a child."

It was his honesty that struck Circe – soft and feminine. He was talking to her as an equal, filled with a respect that she had never experienced from any being, not even Artemis, at least not so instantly.

"Understand us, Circe, we both are here with you willingly." Artemis spoke now, matching the respect from her brother, "We want this world to survive beyond this war, we have chosen our side… with you and the child to be… I too want to pledge my blood to this child."

Circe's mind began to whirr in the way it always did as the final stages of a spell formed into their completion. A twice-blessed child. She turned and waved for Apollo and Artemis to follow her. As she glided through the forest in silence, the twin Gods did the same, watching her with fixed eyes. It was only as they reached the clearing before her house that she stopped and turned to speak. In a deliberate and quiet voice, she said, "You both mean to give your blood willingly, but I need one more promise: an oath of protection. If this works, when my child is born, the world will feel it, Olympus will feel it and I fear their eyes will find me… You must swear on the Styx that you will hide and protect them at any cost. Do you swear it?"

"I do," they replied in unison. The warm tone of Apollo harmonising with the coolness of Artemis.

Circe bid them wait as she gathered everything she needed. When she returned, she held a bowl with a thick, pungent green paste in one hand, and in the other was a goblet filled with a silvery liquid. Circe breezed past the pair, heading straight back up towards the alter from where they had just met, the twin Gods following behind her, both in awe of the deliberateness of the witch before them. Once they reached the altar again, Circe placed the goblet and bowl on the tabletop, blew seven beeswax candles into life and took a deep breath.

"Take the knife on the altar and give your blood to the moon water in the goblet," her instruction came quietly.

Apollo, without hesitation, moved forward, and took the knife in his hand, and cut across his palm. "The blood of Apollo is freely given," he felt compelled to say as his golden ichor dripped thickly into the goblet. Then Artemis stepped forward and did as her brother had done before. She picked up the knife, cut across her palm, and repeated in a similar fashion, "The blood of Artemis is freely given."

Now Circe stepped forward to pick up the goblet, she brought it to her naval as she muttered words of binding and hope. Swiftly, she raised the cup to her mouth and drank it down; it tasted sweet like rich honey. She moved then to put the candles at five points and then gave one to Artemis and bid her stand at one end of the altar and the other to Apollo, and he stood at the other. Both Artemis and Apollo had become quite enthralled watching Circe work her magic, following her every instruction without question.

Slipping out of her dress, she lay atop of the table, her head resting near Artemis. Her hand found the bowl of paste at her side, and she began to paint it on to her stomach, chanting as she did. Slowly, Apollo and Artemis began to join in the chant with her. This was the missing part she hadn't been able to get —the harmony created by their three voices. As they reached the end of the incantation, the flames of the candles leapt tall from their wick, the air rushed around them in a fury, the water in the stream flooded its banks, soaking Apollo's feet, and the earth beneath them rumbled.

It was done.

4

The protective boundary of her island had been reinstated as soon as the ritual between the divine twins had finished, to keep peace of mind from any unwanted godly attention. Artemis and Apollo appeared to have free reign to come and go. Perhaps, she thought, it was the bond between them and the child growing inside her, after all, she hadn't reworked the spell to compensate for them.

The months passed in relative peace. Circe lived as she always had, crafting spells and potions and walking the island, transforming any trespassers into swine and beasts when they came too close to her home. Her mind wandered often to the future of the unborn baby, wondering if the gods might discover her before the birth and if they did what might happen to her.

Apollo would visit a few times a week, announcing his arrival with a crow as white as snow. He brought news of mainland Greece as well as up on Olympus. It eased her worries greatly when he said, in his sweet voice.

"They continue their existence with no thought of you or what might be."

He had become quite fixated on her growing belly, marvelling at the nature of mortal birth. When the baby had begun kicking, Circe had taken his hand and placed it on her round belly. It is not easy to silence a god, but Apollo was mesmerised, speechless at the feeling. When he would leave, Artemis would take his place in the night. Often, she would bring the same tales as Apollo, which in a way served Circe on a deeper level; it helped cement her trust in the twin Gods. Artemis and Circe would lay in bed together and talk, Artemis too marvelling when her hand pressed against the firm stomach of her friend and the movement within.

On the first day of her thirty-eighth week, Circe had just watched a group of sailors set sail from her beach, relieved they hadn't strayed from the sand. They knew the stories of the island they had found themselves on. Helped, she was sure, by the divine twins spreading stories of the terrible witch of Aeaea. She raised her hands in the direction of the boat as it lowered its sail, and muttered an incantation, and watched as the wind caught the sail. She could hear their cheer of good fortune; a smile crossed her face as she cradled her belly. In quiet contentedness, Circe strolled her way back to her home. As she broke the edge of the trees into the clearing, she looked up and noticed the sun and moon were both clear in the sky.

A dull ache rippled through her lower abdomen. She gripped her stomach. Her first contraction. The second came quickly after, and then another. A low groan escaped her mouth. She gripped the door frame, her knuckles white, as she breathed through the pain.

"Artemis? Apollo?" she called out just as another contraction pulsed through her. In the same instant, she felt a warm hand on her left elbow and a cooler hand on her right. They had come, and not a moment too soon.

The twins lowered Circe to the ground before Artemis went to work fetching water and cloths to aid the birth. Apollo, meanwhile, kept by Circe's side, offering words of comfort. Circe's breathing came fast and sharp as she began to push with the encouragement of Artemis.

"Almost there, Circe, be strong and push one more time," Artemis said.

Circe pushed.

It was a moment felt across the entire world. Every living beast and bird let out a great cry to welcome this new life. The sun and moon seemed to pulse with light, and the earth itself shook. Circe felt every inch of magic she had ever encountered surge through her in ecstasy as the first cry came from the babe Artemis had swaddled in fresh cloth.

"You have a son." Artemis couldn't hide the joy from her face. This would be the closest she would ever get to having a child of her own; she could feel that same wildness in the baby that resided in Circe. Handing the mewling babe, she kissed her gently on the forehead. Circe brought him close to her chest seeing nothing but the new baby boy.

"Nicos, my son," Circe kissed the boy's forehead. "You are so loved. What? What is it?"

Circe had looked up to see both Apollo and Artemis staring at the sky.

"Zeus is calling us home. The world felt the birth of Nicos, and the heavens too."

Apollo answered, a tinge of worry dancing on his words, "We have to go."

Circe slowly pulled herself to her feet. One good thing about being the child of a Titan is that you heal quickly. She clutched the now-quiet baby tightly to her and looked at Artemis and Apollo.

"Then go, you must. Thank you for all you have given me. Return to me when you can."

With that said, they were gone. Circe felt the bubble of worry in her core but pushed it away as she gazed adoringly at the new life in her arms.

"You are a twice-blessed child outside of fate, and yet you have a destiny like none before you. I am proud to be your mother."

As the evening crept in, Circe lay Nicos on the bed, then busied herself with some small tasks, stopping now and then to watch the sleeping child. She was about to fix herself something to eat when Artemis burst through the door.

"They are coming! Circe, where is the child?"

"Artemis, steady yourself." Circe answered as she stood following Artemis into the bedroom, "Did you forget my magic keeps…"

"Your wards are not up, Circe! Apollo is buying us time, but we don't have much of it. They don't know about the baby; they think it's just you. Zeus is furious."

The words fell on Circe like knives, "I didn't even… You have come to take Nicos?" The realisation tore her heart into pieces.

"Apollo and I vowed to protect him. I can hide him and raise him well, but we must go now." Artemis waited a moment as she watched Circe pick up Nicos, "My dearest one if I could think of another way…"

Circe kissed the head of her son one last time and handed him over to Artemis. "Be brave, my son, and be strong. Go."

Artemis moved to leave and then turned back, "Goodbye, my dearest one. I…"

"Me too".

Circe stood alone in the bedroom, her heart bursting into a million pieces. It took everything in her not to collapse in on herself. The sudden deafening crash of thunder and flash of lightning forced the witch to steady herself. A deep voice called her name. She inhaled deeply, raised herself to her fullest height, and went to face the king of Olympus.

5

The pantheon of the gods resided at the highest point of Mount Olympus, impossible for any mortal to get near, though some had tried. The palace was an ornate circular room of polished marble edged with twelve great pillars. In the middle of the floor was something that resembled a large mirror, surrounded by twelve thrones made from the wood of cedar trees. Each was adorned with rich fabrics, a different colour for each. Symbols were carved into the back, denoting who sat where.

One stood taller than all the rest, draped in fabric of rich purple and gold, and carved into the back of the seat was a thunderbolt. To its left was another raised throne, only not as high. This too was draped in rich purples and greens, reminiscent of the plume of giant peacock feathers that were in front of each arm, and a lotus was cut into its back. These, of course, belonged to the King and Queen of Olympus, Zeus, and Hera.

Working around clockwise from the throne of Hera came Ares. The emblem of a shield and spear and thick blood red material covered his place, spilling onto the floor, and pooling like blood. Then came a throne draped in fine silks in shades of pink and red. It was perhaps the most inviting of all; a smell of rose lingered in the material, a dove was carved into its back. In comparison, the next seemed hard and cold. A firm-looking, smoky grey cushion lay on the seat, with oily, sooty handprints staining the end of the throne's arms. The Goddess of the Hunt's throne was next, the simplest of all.

The natural cedar wood was left bare with a quiver of arrows leaning against its right-hand side, and a forest green chiffon wrapped itself around the arms like vines. Then came a throne in a small pool of turquoise sea water that had gentle waves lapping against its base. It flowed up into the wood, creating tiny rivers in the grooves. A trident was carved neatly into the back. After this, a seat covered in yellow silk and orange chiffon, giving a sense of frivolity. A lyre was carved into the back, and an actual lyre of turtle shell rested on the seat.

A small table stood next to the throne to the left of Apollo with two jugs of wine, one white and one red, a simple bronze goblet, and bunches of grapes of a deep purple that matched the swathes of purple silk that muddled with silks of rich red. Up next came a place marked with a scythe and a wheat sheaf. Spring green chiffon flowed from the top to black as it touched the floor. The last two thrones belonged to Hermes and Athena.

First came the messenger of the gods, simple black fabric wrapped itself around the left arm, whilst the right was in a brilliant blue. His winged staff with two snakes was engraved on the back. Finally, at Zeus' right hand was the throne of Athena, Goddess of Wisdom and Strategy. A delicate white silk-covered cushion was on the seat, with white feather-like material spilling from underneath it like milk. An owl marked her space and so completed the circle of Olympian thrones.

There had been few times when all the gods had been summoned at one time by Zeus, save to watch the outcome of a war between the mortals, from whom they had all taken sides for fun. Now they had all been gathered for a much deeper concern.

Zeus sat tall on his throne, a mane of stormy grey hair falling just past his shoulders. His lightning-blue eyes looked fierce in his bearded face as they stared fixedly at the mirror before him on the floor. Only now it showed the mortal world below, focusing on the area near the Ionian Sea. Hera followed his eyes with her own deep violet ones, scanning for something that she too could not see. She was unquestionably beautiful; it came from her regal propriety. She stood straight-backed, never hunching or slouching, and moved every part of her body with deliberate grace. Her face held high cheek bones and a mouth sporting two full lips. Falling to the base of her spine was thick, wavy black hair with two peacock feathers braided in.

Soft footfalls fell on the cool marble floor, and hushed, hurried chatter signalled the arrival of the other immortals. Aphrodite was first, accompanied by her husband, Hephaestus; the two looked odd together. She was a tall woman with a full-bodied hourglass figure that moved with effortless sensuality, vibrant long blonde hair, and bright green eyes that were flecked with gold.

Hephaestus was tall himself, though he stood a few inches shorter than his wife due to his slightly hunched back. His dark hair was cropped short, and his beard was full and slightly unkempt. A great scar ran through his right eye that he never allowed to heal; he wanted it to serve as a reminder to his mother, Hera, after all, she was the one who threw him down the side of Olympus when he was born. He was the only immortal to have these imperfections. They greeted Zeus and Hera as they took their seats.

Ares came in seconds later, dressed in black and gold armour. He removed his red-plumed helmet as he approached his father, revealing jet black hair and dark eyes.

"Father," Ares voice was rough, "Mother".

The water at the base of Poseidon's throne began to whip into a frenzy, cascading up to a great height before collapsing down again to reveal the handsome figure of the Sea God, Poseidon, trident in hand. Poseidon looked younger than his brother Zeus, even though his hair was as white as seafoam. He had turquoise eyes and a cold expression, his dark skin was flecked with blues and greens. Athena had taken her seat, entering the Olympian palace almost unnoticed.

She had already fixed her grey eyes on the sprawling world below, whispering things to Zeus, who murmured in response. It was no secret to any of the gods that Athena was his favoured child. Dionysus and Demeter arrived, offering their greetings before sitting down quickly. Zeus looked up and noticed three empty seats. His brow furrowed. Hermes, he thought, was probably being detained by his brother Hades, but then where were the twins? No sooner had the thought begun to form in his head, both Artemis and Apollo appeared side by side. Both bowed and took their places. Zeus stood, silencing the last of the chatter. All eyes fixed on the king.

"It has been sometime since all of the family were gathered together." Zeus' voice was soft with a threatening rumble, like distant thunder. "I will not waste time; we all fe…"

Hermes sped into the room with a sound like hummingbird wings. "Forgive my interruption, father, but Hades sends his apologies. I am to report back to him with all we discuss… if that pleases you."

"Very well," he gestured for Hermes to sit. "Moments ago, a great disturbance was felt across all of Greece. It shook the earth…"

"Not of my doing, dear brother," Poseidon interrupted.

"And the beasts, all of them, in the same moment, cried out," Zeus continued. "Does anyone have an explanation?"

No one spoke.

"I would ask now that each of you turn your eyes to the world and help me discover what is the cause." Each divine being leant forward, scanning the world before them for anything out of the ordinary. Artemis saw it first, and her eyes darted up to find Apollo looking to her; he too had seen it. Circe's island. It was there, laid bare in the Ionian Sea; it was only a matter of time before someone else noticed it.

I have to warn her and protect the child, thought Artemis.

Apollo nodded, *We have to do this right, give nothing away. Wait for my signal, dear sister.*

Artemis gave a small nod and returned her gaze.

"There," Athena's cool voice cut through the silence, "that island is new, or rather, I haven't seen it for the longest time."

"Is it not Aeaea? The home of that Titan runt, Ceris?" Ares said.

"Circe." Hera corrected. She looked at her husband and noticed the smallest flash of panic in Zeus' eyes.

"I thought she was dead," Dionysus remarked as he took a gulp of wine.

"The witch who held the gods at bay now reveals herself. Can it be a coincidence?" Aphrodite asked.

With a wave of his great hand, the world was gone, and the mirror rested clear again. Zeus paced back and forth as the other Olympians whispered. Apollo moved to his sister and squeezed her hand.

"This witch has gone unchecked long enough!" Zeus rumbled, "It acts as though it were a god! I will go to Aeaea myself and scorch her from this earth."

"Wait, father," Apollo shouted. He felt all the eyes of the gods upon him. Steadying himself, he continued, "It could be a trap. Why would she reveal herself in such a way if not to lure us in?"

"You think she could best me, Apollo?" Zeus roared.

"No… maybe," Apollo answered, "She is a child of a Titan with a magic that we Olympians cannot undo, and now she announces herself so boldly; to what end?"

"I am the mighty Zeus and will not be bested by a runt offspring of a Titan god!" His voice shook the floor.

Apollo stepped forward, swallowing his fear of the rage building in his father. "Hear me, father, you are indeed powerful, but… this witch kept us all at bay. I fear her power." Apollo flicked his eyes at Artemis, *GO NOW,* he thought, and she was gone, unnoticed. "Should we not take some precaution? Find out what she is up to."

"Apollo may have a point, Zeus," It was Athena who spoke, her cool voice tempering the brewing storm within her father. "Perhaps we should face her with a strategy."

"Oh whatever," laughed Ares, "Zeus has a plan! Go in and destroy the bitch. Simple."

"Brute force isn't always the answer, especially when one desires information," Athena scolded.

"What answers do we need? Really, Athena, you are so precious, it is a wonder you are ever associated with the brilliance of war." Ares answered.

"You dim-witted bastard. Could it even cross your tiny mind that she maybe up to something bigger?"

"Enough!" Hera commanded in a powerful voice, "Ares and Athena are both right; Apollo too. Zeus, it is clear Circe must be dealt with, but if there is more afoot here, then we must get answers."

Zeus considered his options before answering calmly, though his lightning danced about his fingers. "Athena, you will come with me, Ares too, though be warned, boy, if you disobey me or act out, you will be sorry. You are all free to do as you wish for now." In a great crack of lightning, Zeus, Athena, and Ares were gone, and so was Apollo.

***

Artemis held the sleeping Nicos close, breath tight in her chest, as she stepped on to the peak of Mount Kynthos on the island of her birth, Delos. Apollo was there, waiting. He greeted her with a solemn smile. Artemis handed him the baby, and she watched as he laid him down on some furs that had been arranged into a sort of bed. The twins stepped away towards the edge of the mountainside and stared out into the crisp night sky. Nothing was said for a long time, they just stood side by side. Apollo took hold of Artemis' hand, holding it tight, as they watched a fierce and violent storm rage in the distance.

"Are you alright, sister?" Apollo spoke gently.

"Yes," Artemis answered, although the quietness of her voice betrayed her truth. "What shall we do with the boy?"

"We honour our oath. Though we cannot keep him with us, that much is clear. Zeus will be placated for a while with the de…," he said, catching himself at the look of sorrow in his sister's eyes. "Well, he will be placated for a while. It gives us time." He knelt beside the sleeping Nicos, gently running a finger over his cheek. "I had forgotten how small the mortals are when they are born."

"We will hide him with my hunters in Attica; they occupy a forest there and are my most devoted." Artemis spoke as she knelt next to Nicos, watching his peaceful sleeping face. "I have never questioned our fathers' decisions before, not intensely anyway, but after tonight, something has changed in me."

Apollo sighed heavily, "I know, I feel it to. Perhaps this is the beginning of the war. We will not be the only ones who question his judgement, and we know there is more to come. You must take Nicos to your hunters for now. I will return to Olympus on our behalf." Apollo kissed the sleeping boy's forehead and got to his feet. Artemis stood to embrace her brother. He kissed her cheek and was gone. She stooped down and picked up Nicos.

In a moment, her feet fell silently on the forest floor in Attica, where she was greeted by a great brown stag. It bowed to her, and she, smiling, returned the bow before climbing up on its back, the child held tightly in her arms. They took off through the rich green forest as the light of dawn began to break through the trees. Deeper and deeper they went. Artemis could see her destination ahead, so she urged the stag to a standstill before gracefully dismounting. In thanks, she pressed her forehead against the stags. She looked down to check on the still-sleeping child, marvelling at him.

"Your mother was the greatest friend I have ever known. I will protect you and love you as fiercely as I did her." Artemis kissed his cheek before taking the final few steps into the hunters' village.

The settlement was made up of twenty or so small homes, each made of wood with doors covered by animal hides. It had a central raised platform atop which stood a statue of Artemis, bow in hand, aiming at something unseen. Artemis moved silently to the centre of the settlement and sat under her statue, waiting with Nicos for the hunters to awaken. As they waited, Nicos at some point, opened his eyes and began to cry.

"Sweet boy, be calm. Though much has happened in your short life, know that you have the Goddess Artemis on your side and the God Apollo too." His crying softened as she rocked him back to sleep.

The crying, however, had woken the sleeping hunters. They wandered out to find the source of the noise. The women were dressed in deep forest greens, and some already had their bows strapped to their backs. Artemis stood to meet them. Instantly, they fell to their knees.

"You, take this child from me." Artemis waved over a young woman with short blonde hair. "Where is Thea?" Artemis asked. A tall, dark-skinned woman arose from the gathering, her eyes of deep hazel locked with the fierce yellow eyes of Artemis.

"I am here, great Artemis." Thea answered in a voice that could only belong to a leader. The goddess broke out into a smile.

"My friend, you look well."

"As do you, my goddess". Thea bowed respectfully before kissing the hand of Artemis, "What brings you to us after so long away?" Her eyes darted to the baby being fed some goats milk by the young woman who had taken him.

"I will take a walk with you, come." Artemis turned and moved silently into the forest, with Thea following behind her, not daring to speak. When they were a short distance away from the village, Artemis said, "Everything I am about to ask of you is more than I have ever done before, and I do so because I trust you and my hunters completely. Do you understand?"

Thea nodded.

"I need you to take care of the child. It is important that no one outside of the village knows he is here or that I was the one who brought him. He has a destiny that will shape the world, but some see him as a threat. But without him… Teach him well. I will be close by as always, as will my brother Apollo. If you cannot fulfil this, then speak now." Artemis finished speaking and watched the woman before her as she processed everything; she admired her calmness.

"Of course, we will do this. We will raise him in the way of the hunt and nurture him as our own. Does he have a name?" Thea asked.

"Nicos."

"Nicos is a strong name. If the boy should ask about his parentage and past, what would you have us tell him?"

Artemis pondered this. "Tell him that he is the son of a powerful witch, and I shall do the rest when the time is right. I must return now to Olympus; be wise, Thea, and know you and all the hunters are blessed and will be blessed again by Artemis."

Before Thea could reply, the Goddess of the Hunt was gone, and she was left alone with the weight of all that had been said. Thea made her way back to the village to find the other women in deep conversation about Artemis and the child. She made her way to the young blonde woman, still holding the boy.

"Pass him to me, Korinna." With the baby in her arms, she moved on top of the raised platform and addressed her people. "Hunters of Artemis, we have been chosen by our great goddess to raise this child as our own. No one can know who brought him here. Nicos is one of us, and you will lay down your life to protect him. We will teach him the ways of the hunt."

A cheer erupted from the gathered women, and Nicos was embraced into the hunters of Artemis.

6

The boy's childhood passed with peace and ease. Each and every woman who made up the hunters became to him a mother. They took pride in teaching him the ways of the hunt, though it was Thea and Korinna he was closest to of all. Thea taught him how to handle a bow and arrow, which Nicos took to like a duck to water. His skill was natural, effortless. Many remarked that he was indeed blessed by Artemis. Korinna noticed the boy's innate understanding of plants early, so she taught him medicines and the art of healing.

By the time he was in his early teens, Nicos, however, had begun teaching Korinna. New concoctions came to him in his dreams —a salve that soothed and healed burns overnight. A draught that could send you into a death like sleep, a brew that would sharpen your eyesight in the dark of night, and many others. Nicos also had an uncanny ability to communicate with animals. Cora, a strong-muscled hunter who looked after the horses, had watched Nicos tame the wildest of their herd when he was just nine years old. There was also the chimaera.

The hunters had been called upon by a nearby village to help with a dangerous chimaera, which had decided to make its home in a nearby cave. At fourteen, Nicos was lean, with a mop of forest brown hair streaked through with copper. His eyes were rich hazel, flecked with green and gold. This wasn't his first hunt by any means, but it was one of the more treacherous. Nicos was crouched close behind Thea, who was just in front of him, a knife in hand. She motioned for him to move forward. The opening of the cave stood before them, beyond the trees from where they were covered.

"Do you see it?" Nicos whispered as he moved next to Thea.

"Not yet… I'll lure it out. Be ready with your bow. I will signal the others." Thea moved out of cover and stood up tall in front of the cave entrance. She raised her hand and, hidden from sight, the other hunters notched an arrow into place and waited. Nicos began to follow suit, but suddenly his eyes weren't his own. He was seeing the woods from deeper within, and he was moving quickly. Branches and leaves whipped past his face. Surely, he should feel the sting of them cutting his cheek. He recognised something about the woods; it was the same route they had taken not many minutes before. Then, in an instant, he was back to seeing with his own eyes again.

"Thea!" Nicos burst from the cover of the treeline.

"Nicos, get back now!"

"Listen to me, it's not in there! The chimaera… It's coming from that direction; we don't have long." He pointed back the way they had come.

"Nicos, how…?" Thea knew better than to question how he knew. "Hunters, with me now!"

In seconds, the ten other hunters had emerged and formed into a protective semicircle blocking the entrance of the chimaeras' cave. Nicos raised his bow and pulled the string tight, an arrow aimed dead ahead, ready to fire. A roar rippled through the woodland before the great beast burst forward into view. It was a sight to behold, and Nicos was as mesmerised as much as he was terrified.

The head and body of a lion at its front, with a goat's head protruding from its back. Black goat legs for its backend, and finally, its great tail was scaled and ended with the head of a snake. It was huge. Flames teased out of the chimaeras lion mouth as it fixed its gaze upon the flesh before it.

"Hold," Thea commanded.

Each hunter had their bowstring pulled tight and the feathers of the arrow ends rested against their cheeks. The chimaera padded closer, black eyes scanning each piece of prey in its way. It let out a low growl and made to pounce.

"NOW!!!"

A volley of arrows whipped toward the monster. Most of them made their target, piercing into the furry body, causing it to rear onto its hind legs, fire erupting out of its mouth. As it came back down to all fours with a thud, the fire scorched three hunters on the right. They dropped their weapons as they fell screaming to the floor. With a cue from Thea, two more hunters ran to aid their fallen sisters, whilst the rest shot fresh arrows at the chimaera. As they pierced its body again, the chimaera charged forward, seemingly unphased. With its great clawed paw, it swept aside four more of the women, sending them flying into trees, save one, who was sent into the rock of the cave entrance with a deadly crunch. Nicos could feel the fear rising in him, but he knew he must keep a handle on it, the way his many mothers had taught him.

"Nicos, run! Go!" Thea ordered as she turned to face the chimaera.

"I won't leave you!" Nicos answered.

His heart pounded in his chest as he watched Thea release arrow after arrow until she reached back to find her quiver empty. She threw the bow aside and pulled out her kopis. The curved blade caught the sun as she held it aloft at the beast. Nicos shot his remaining arrows, the chimaera let out a bust of fire as they came towards it, turning them to ash. Thea ran forward at the distracted animal, ready to plunge her dagger into its side, but it turned and swatted her aside with its snake tail. Thea was sent soaring. She landed with a thud at the mouth of the cave, winded. The chimaera stalked forward towards her. Nicos ran as fast as he ever had and slid across the floor to put himself between Thea and the chimaera. He took Thea's kopis and watched as the terrifying creature stopped. It was so close he could feel the heat of its breath on his face; it felt like it was blistering.

"Artemis," Thea pleaded in a whisper behind Nicos.

"You will not have my mother!" Nicos shouted as he got to his feet, the curved blade still pointed forward. The chimaera cocked its head at his words; if he didn't know any better, he would have said it understood him. The heat lessened on his face. A growl answered him as the chimaera seemed to soften before him. Nicos' brow furrowed. Thea felt her breath catch tighter in her chest as she watched Nicos begin to lower the kopis.

"Artemis please!" She pleaded again as tears formed in her eyes. A coolness touched her as Artemis appeared just behind, her bow already aimed, but she didn't take the shot. She watched as Nicos moved closer to the chimaera.

The beast and the young hunter stared at each other, passing unspoken words. Nicos extended his hand out. A long moment of silence and stillness followed before the chimaera pressed its cheek to his palm. Artemis lowered her bow, awestruck. Thea gasped as she was helped to her feet. Nicos petted the chimaera as though it were as harmless as a cat. The hunters, battered and bruised, had slowly gathered themselves by Thea and Artemis, watching the taming of the chimaera with wonder.

The chimaera's eyes flicked up from Nicos, snapping him back to the present situation. His heart swelled as he turned to see Thea on her feet with the other hunters, except one who still lay motionless at the mouth of the cave.

Artemis caught his eyes, she smiled, stepping forward to say, "Nicos, tamer of chimaera, you are indeed a proud addition to my hunters."

Dropping to his knees, Nicos replied, "Thank you, mighty Artemis."

"There is no need to kneel before me; stand. Tell me, what should we do with this beast?" Artemis asked in her usual cool tone.

"I gave my word that I would do no harm if she didn't, and so I cannot kill her, nor will I." Nicos said.

"You would let it live even after it has killed many before and one of your own today?" Artemis queried.

Nicos looked at the still body of Malva, for that is who had been killed. She had taught him how to fish, from catching to filleting. She was kind, he thought. "A life for a life does not always make things right." Nicos bowed his head, a little embarrassed.

Artemis touched her hand under the boy's chin and lifted his head, "Do not hide your face in shame. I knew another who respected the life of beasts; she was a great woman. I ask you again, though, what should we do with the beast?"

"Is there somewhere we could take her that she might live freely and safely? Away from humans?" Nicos asked.

A smile teased at the corners of Artemis' mouth, "I know of an island where I can take your friend."

"Thank you," Nicos beamed.

Artemis raised her arms up; the chimaera was gone, as too was the Goddess of the Hunt. Nicos ran forward to Thea and embraced her tightly, causing her to wince in pain. In silence, he and a couple of the hunters who were able to gathered the body of Malva and began to make their way back home.

The journey back was quiet. No one dared to speak especially, it seemed, to Nicos. He rode silently beside Thea as his mind busied itself with thoughts about all that had come to pass. Beside the taming of the chimaera, he had just met the Goddess of the Hunt herself in person. Why had she come? She was beautiful and powerful, and he had spoken with her. Then she had done as he had asked. It was as though he were a friend asking a simple favour. A smile crept across his teenage face. Thea looked over at him, and he lost his smile. She tried to say something but instead held her tongue.

It was early dusk as they finally reached the stables of their village. All the warriors wearily dismounted from their steeds. A rider had been sent ahead to announce that Malva had been killed and a burial was to be made ready. Nicos helped carry the body up to its final resting place and laid her down with her hunting bow. He knelt and said goodbye to the warrior woman before moving through the crowd to find Korinna. Nicos found her near the back of the assembled crowd. She pulled him into a tight, motherly hug. Finally, tears escaped his eyes as he clung tightly back.

Thea, however, had taken her place at the front and turned now to speak to her clan, "My dear ones, today we lost our sister Malva. It is always hard to say goodbye. We commend her now to Hades; may you find your way to Elysium." Thea placed a gold coin inside Malva's mouth. Then Antonia, the priestess, came forward to anoint the body with perfumes. Thea and Antonia covered her in white linen as the gathered women offered prayers to Hades that he would welcome their sister.

As Antonia threw the first hand of dirt on to the body, she said, "Hades, great King of the Underworld, may you take this hunter of Artemis and see her find peace evermore," Antonia's voice was filled with sorrow and solemnity. As they finished burying Malva proper, Korinna took Nicos by the hand and led him back towards their home.

Nicos recounted everything to Korinna as they walked. Not once did she interrupt or show any emotion on her face. Even after he finished, she still didn't speak. A pit of worry had settled in his stomach. He had known he was different from most people around him, but he had never felt different — not really, not until now. Korinna leant against their front door and looked at Nicos, observing the fourteen-year-old boy before her. She saw his worry and put her hand to his cheek, noticing then the blistered burn on it.

"I have just the thing for this," she smiled. "Light the fire. I will be back in a moment," Korinna disappeared into the small house as Nicos gathered some wood and built a fire in the pit in front of the house.

Thea came up to the home as Nicos started to light the fire. He gave her a weak smile, which she did not return and went inside. He could hear their voices coming from inside, and although he knew he shouldn't, he tried hard to hear what was being said. It was no use as he only could hear the odd word like "chimaera", "Artemis", "witch" and "truth". He focused again on lighting the fire as he heard their footsteps coming towards the door. Nicos sat on the ground, facing the flames, as Thea and Korinna came to join him. Korinna immediately got to rubbing the burn salve on Nicos' right cheek; her touch was gentle.

"Are you okay?" Thea asked honestly.

"It's a light burn; I am fine." Nicos replied coldly.

"Lose the tone, Nicos," Korinna chided.

Thea took a deep breath, "Forgive me, for I have not known what to say. A lot has happened to you, me, and, well, all of us. I first should thank you…"

"For what?" Nicos turned to face her and was moved to see her looking straight back at him.

"Saving my life. There is much we want to tell you, Nicos, but… What you did today was extraordinary. You had no idea you could do that?" Thea moved to sit on his other side.

Nicos stared at the flames before him again, "No, well… maybe."

The three of them sat quietly as the light of the fire danced on their faces. Above, the Grecian sky danced with stars, and the crescent moon added a silver shimmer to the night. Korinna squeezed Nicos' hand.

"It isn't the first time, and I dare say it won't be the last. Perhaps it is something we can work on and understand." She always knew how to ease his worries.

"Why did Artemis show?" Nicos asked Thea.

"I called to her."

"Why?"

"Because of you. After all, it was she who brought you to us, which you know. She came to aid you when I could not." Thea spoke softly. Nicos took both of her hands in his and gave them a small squeeze.

"Thank you."

7

The years after the chimaera passed amongst the hunters, as they always had, they spent time training, hunting, and helping villages in need. If a beast was involved, then sure enough, Nicos was guaranteed to be asked along. Rumours slowly began to spread throughout Greece about the hunter of Artemis, who could tame the monstrous beasts with the touch of a hand. Thea had members of the tribe keep track on any whisperings when they were at markets or dealing with other Grecians. She wanted to make sure that Nicos was never mentioned as a man, for it would draw too much attention.

Thea had risen early and meandered her way through the hunters' village to the statue of Artemis. She sat, closed her eyes, and offered her usual morning prayer of thanks. Birds of the forest started to trill their morning songs, making Thea smile as she sat listening to it floating on the crisp morning air. A deep feeling of contentedness filled her at the sounds of the other women starting their day. She heard someone approach before a hand lightly touched her shoulder. She opened her eyes to see Hermia.

"Forgive me for intruding on you, Thea," Hermia said as she crouched down next to Thea.

"What is it Hermia?" Thea asked warmly.

Hermia took a breath before saying clearly and quickly, "I was at the Agora in Athens, and there was talk of a male amongst our tribe. It was disputed by a few, but it gained some traction, I stepped in to dispel any belief in it. It would seem that Nicos' anonymity may be jeopardised."

"We have made it almost to his eighteenth year before any hint at discovery…" Thea's brow furrowed in thought, "I want you to go back and take some of the others with you to see if you can't diffuse this rumour before it spreads too far. Do what you can."

Hermia nodded and made to leave before stopping herself and saying, "There was something else… The Oracle of Delphi was speaking of a twice-blessed child, a war between gods, and it is said Apollo himself showed and silenced her by taking her tongue." She turned on her heel heading to find companions to take back to Athens. Thea's head whirled. How quickly the feeling of peace had left her. She pressed her hands to the feet of the statue beside her.

"Artemis, it seems our time is up. I will bring Nicos to the river clearing, and with you there or not, I will tell him all I know." Thea arose and moved quickly towards her home.

As she hurried back, she noticed the faces of some of the women and knew that Hermia had spread word of what had happened. Good, she thought; it was one less thing she needed to explain. As Thea rounded the corner, she saw Nicos and Korinna busying themselves over a workbench in front of their home. A sharp pang of guilt caught in her chest as she watched them both laugh. Thea felt her heart break. She knew one day she would lose him to his destiny, but she hadn't prepared herself for how much she would grow to love him, as deeply as if he were her own son.

"Thea!" Nicos beamed as she came up beside him, putting her arm around his shoulders. "Korinna and I thought we might go foraging this morning. Will you join us?"

"Actually, I need you to go and ready our horses," Thea said.

Nicos looked from Thea to Korinna, who smiled, nodding for him to go. He kissed them both on the cheek and ran off towards the stables. Thea looked to Korinna and could feel the tears burning her eyes, without a word being said, Korinna understood and pulled Thea to her, holding her as she let the tears fall.

"Will you tell him anything on your ride?" Korinna asked as she put some bread and figs into a satchel before putting it on Thea's shoulder. She shook her head in reply. Korinna tucked her fingers under Thea's chin, making her look her in the eye, "We knew this day would come. He is strong because of us. You must promise me one thing, however."

"What?" Thea answered.

"Don't let her take him before he can come back and say goodbye to us all." Korinna said firmly.

"I will do my best. I promise."

They walked together to find Nicos in the paddock between two horses, both bridled and saddled. It dawned on both women how much he had grown. He stood now at a perfect six feet. His body was lean, and he moved with effortless grace. His hair, which he often pulled into a ponytail, fell below his shoulders. His face had lost all traces of childishness. Nicos was striking to behold. Thea often marvelled at how he danced the line between masculine and feminine in his features and movements. Both attributes lived within him in harmonious duality. When he caught sight of

Thea and Korinna, he led the two horses forward to meet them.

"Where are we headed?" Nicos asked as he passed the reigns of a rich liver chestnut mare named Zephyra to Thea. She pulled herself up onto the horse and gave its neck a pat.

"The river clearing," Thea replied, "I would like to get there before tomorrow, so hurry up and mount". She grinned.

Nicos gave Korinna a kiss on the cheek, and she pulled him close to her. She held him tight as though she may never let go, but she did, desperately trying to hide the tears forming in her eyes.

"What is it?" Nicos asked.

Korinna waved him off. "I will see you later, and we can forage tomorrow."

Nicos warm smile spread across his face as he pulled himself onto his horse with ease. Nicos' horse was the largest in the hunter's stable, with a sleek black coat that shimmered in the light. Thea had headed off and already disappeared into the trees ahead.

"Come, Theron," he spurred the horse on, following closely behind Thea and Zephyra.

For an hour or so, they rode in silence, with Thea keeping a decent distance between herself and Nicos. Keeping the river on their left, they followed it up toward the clearing, halfway up the mountainside. The silence didn't bother Nicos too much as he was used to riding in silence, especially when Thea clearly had something on her mind. He used this time to name wild plants as ideas of potions formed in his mind, or he practiced sharing eyes, as he had come to call it, with Theron or any animals he could feel nearby. Sharing eyes with a warbler, he flew past Thea and could see worry etched on her face. Letting his eyes come back to himself, he asked Theron to catch up to her. Theron did as he was asked and fell into stride with Zephyra.

"What's wrong?" Nicos asked.

"Hmm?" Thea had clearly been lost in thought, "Oh nothing, sweet boy."

Nicos scoffed, "Wasn't it you who taught me not to lie?" He smirked. "Ok, simpler question, why are we going to the clearing?"

"Because…" Thea trailed off and kicked Zephyra into a gallop, sprinting forward into the trees, "Keep up if you can, Nicos," she shouted back over her shoulder.

Nicos couldn't help but laugh as he whispered into Theron's ear to run as fast as he could. Which he did. He could see the behind of Zephyra, not too far ahead. Theron gained speed. If Nicos hadn't heard the hoofs thudding into the forest floor, he might have thought he was flying. It wasn't long until he overtook Thea, who looked amazed as he charged past.

"Keep up if you can, Thea!" Nicos taunted as the distance grew between them. Theron kept going faster and faster. He broke into the river clearing, Theron skidded to a halt, and Nicos dismounted smoothly.

"Well done, my friend," he said as he patted the sweaty flank of the horse before removing his saddle and bridle. The horse gave a shake and a whinny in gratitude and stepped up to the river's edge to drink deeply. Nicos slipped his bare feet into the water and sighed at its coolness. Behind him he heard Zephyra trot into the clearing, with Thea landing almost soundlessly onto the short grass. Zephyra came to drink next to Theron, whilst Thea sat beside Nicos to dip her feet into the water. They both sat there, side by side, drinking in the scent of wildflowers and the faint chirping of birds in the trees overhead.

"Why are we here, Thea?" asked Nicos earnestly.

"Because... the rumour of a male hunter has reached Athens, and I fear your time with us is coming to an end." Thea took hold of Nicos' hand. "You have been with us since you were a babe, and I see you as my son, as do all our tribe, but you have a destiny, and it is time you knew who you are."

"I know who I am. I am Nicos, son of the hunters of Artemis. I do not need to be more." Nicos said, a whisper of pain danced on his words.

"But that is not all you are..." Thea stopped talking as Nicos had brought a finger to his full lips to silence her. She tried to hear what he was hearing. There was nothing. There was no sound at all. The birds had all fallen silent, and their horses had become alert and still. Nicos pointed towards the trees, where he could see something moving towards them. A stag. A huge stag and something, or rather, someone on its back. He moved to get his bow and arrow and aimed steadily in the direction of the approaching beast. It surprised him when Thea pushed his arm down.

"Thea?"

"Nicos, I asked them to be here."

Thea bowed her head a little as the stag stepped out of the trees. It was the largest stag Nicos had ever seen. It oozed an ethereal nobility. He was so stunned at the beauty of the animal it took him a moment to recognise the deity astride it. In fact, it wasn't until she slipped silently off the back and came to stand beside it that Nicos noticed who it was. Artemis. He drank in the sight of her, tall, striking, and wild.

Her great yellow eagle eyes fixed on him; a delicate smile lighting up her face. She whispered something to the stag, who then offered her a bow before it turned to run back into the forest.

Thea went up and greeted her friend, and both made quiet conversation. Every now and again, one or both of them would look over at Nicos.

"It's rude to talk about someone when they are in same place." He said as he set his bow back down and returned the arrow to its quiver.

Artemis let out a laugh that rippled through the air before turning her face back to Thea, and they carried on. Nicos sighed and turned his back on them both, busying himself by looking into the stream, trying to distract himself from the unsettled feeling that rested in his stomach. It felt like an age before he heard the soft, almost silent footfalls approaching him. He stood to face the two women.

"It is good to see you again, Nicos, the chimaera tamer." Artemis said. If he didn't know any better, he would have said she spoke with pride in her voice as she addressed him. Nicos bowed his head in answer. "You have grown much since we last met," she said, moving around him and inspecting him. "You look so much like her."

"Who?" Nicos asked.

"The greatest witch who ever lived. Your mother, Circe." Artemis looked at Thea and could see the shock on her face. There wasn't a person alive in Greece who hadn't heard of the cursed witch of Aeaea. The woman who transformed men into beasts. The hag that seduced Odysseus and then had one of their children kill him. Only, it seemed, Nicos had never heard of her, after all, he had never left the camp except with the hunters, and when he had gone near others, he never spoke as he was instructed.

"Start a fire, Thea, I can see now there is much to tell you… both of you."

Thea grabbed Nicos by the wrist and bid him help her set a fire. He moved silently next to her gathering wood, and when they had enough, he made to light it, but Artemis stepped up and waved her hand over the pile of wood, and it burst into flame.

"A trick," she said, "I learnt from my brother."

All three sat as the sky above changed to the rich purples and pinks of dusk. Artemis began. She told of the mighty Circe and how men and gods had painted her as wicked, as they were prone to do of any powerful woman. Nicos was enthralled. Suddenly, parts of life that seemed odd made sense; he had underestimated the comfort that would come from knowing where his gifts came from.

"So," Nicos interrupted, "then you and Apollo gave your blood willingly?"

"Yes. I trusted your mother. Everything she said has come to pass. It is clear you have in you the gifts of your mother and indeed myself–your ability with a bow and your sight even in the darkness." Artemis beamed with pride again. "Though I am yet to see what you got from my brother. You are a being outside of fate, Nicos, something that has never been before. Even we gods are not without our fate."

"The war to come, is that because of me?" Nicos asked, trying hard to understand the whirl of information that now whirled around his mind. A war, gods, witches, and him amongst it all, yet free of fate. How could he be free of something if the fate of all others relied on him?

Artemis considered her reply before saying, "The war was always going to happen, but I do believe that your birth set things in motion faster than perhaps if you had not been born. After Zeus' battle with Circe, he returned, for want of a better description… afraid. It planted a seed of fear and distrust in him of beings with divine blood. Not his direct lineage, of course, but any of our offspring were a threat to him." A great weight seemed to land on Nicos' chest. Thea could see the worry fill the child she had raised for the last eighteen years, she moved to put her arm around him.

"Keep breathing and stay steady in yourself, sweet boy," Thea whispered as she felt him rest into her. Artemis watched as a stab of pain struck her heart. She cared for this boy so much more than she had ever wanted to realise. It was some time before anyone spoke again. The sky now was dotted with stars, and the sounds of the stream drifted calmly on the night air.

Thea broke the silence to ask, "The Oracle of Delphi; did her words reach Zeus' ear?"

Artemis inhaled deeply, "Ah yes, the Oracle. Apollo silenced them by taking their tongue; although I support his actions, he was foolish in his execution. Sadly, the words had been spoken, and their damage had been done. Zeus, I think, hasn't heard what the Oracle said, but it is only a matter of time, especially with Apollo's actions. That is why it is imperative we move Nicos now, whilst he still has his anonymity." Artemis stood and pulled Nicos up by the elbow.

"Wait? What?" Nicos asked in alarm.

"You can't just take him," Thea stood in defiance and pulled Nicos back to her.

"No mortal tells me what I can and cannot do". Artemis turned, irked at Thea's disobedience.

"No! How dare you! Forgive my boldness, Artemis, but you are out of line. You are my goddess, and I have followed you since I was a child and have done as you asked without question, but I will not allow you to take my son."

"He is not your son!" Artemis scolded, her temper flaring.

"He is!!!" Thea shouted back, "I may not have given birth to him or given blood, but I have raised him and loved him as if I had! All the hunters, *your* hunters, have become his mother. You will not deny us the right to say goodbye!"

"Nor will you deny me." Nicos spoke up as he put himself between them. "I will go anywhere you ask after."

Artemis was momentarily stunned at the defiance; all she could do was stare at the two mortals before her. It was rare for any mortal to defy a god and live to tell the tale. With a heavy sigh, she conceded. She flicked her wrist, and a roll of parchment appeared in her hand.

"This is a map to Chiron; you must set off as soon as you can and tell no one of your destination or who you are." Nicos nodded his understanding and took the map in his slightly trembling hand.

"I must return now to Olympus." Her eyes looked up to the heavens. "Be brave, Nicos, for all that is to come. I am always close by." Artemis' final words danced on the night air as she vanished out of sight. In an instant, Nicos had thrown his arms around Thea, who pulled him in close to her. They stayed like this for a while before Nicos' tense body relaxed a little. It took them little time to get both horses saddled and mounted.

In a moment, he had learnt the truth of who his birth mother was and that he was crucial in the outcome of a war between the gods that was yet to be. On top of all that, he had to leave the only family he had ever known and venture into the world —a world he had never really experienced alone. From time to time, he tried to say something, but words failed him, so they carried on under the canopy of trees to sounds of the huffing of the horses and the creatures of the night. It was only when they had made it back to the hunter's settlement and returned their horses to the paddock that anything was said between the pair.

"My son... go and get some rest. You have a long day ahead of you tomorrow. I need to ready a few things ahead of your leaving us," Thea said, her voice wavered slightly.

Nicos pulled her into a tight embrace and whispered, "I love you."

"And I love you."

Nicos raised his fingers to wipe away some silent tears that traced their way down Thea's cheek. She straightened herself, took a deep breath, and then headed towards the village centre. Nicos watched her walk away. Then he made his way back to his home for what could be the last time. Korinna was still awake; it was evident she had waited up for them. She was relieved to see Nicos coming towards her as a smile lit up her face. That was all it took to send him over the edge.

At the sight of her, Nicos felt the tears burst from his eyes, and he ran as fast as he could into the arms of the woman before him. She held him tightly as he talked her through everything that had happened, finishing by telling her that he was going to be leaving them. Korinna listened quietly, and then, when he had done, she took him inside and laid him on the bed, stroking his long hair until sleep finally took over him. Silently, Korinna stood and made her way outside, closing the door behind her. She leant her back against the door as she began to cry. She allowed herself a few moments to digest her feelings before steadying herself and made off to find Thea.

8

Nicos woke up to an empty house and the first rays of morning light spilling through the window. For a moment, he had forgotten that anything had changed, and his life was exactly as it had been. But then the memory of the night before flooded his mind. Nothing was as it was before. With a great effort, Nicos got up out of his bed, changed out of the clothes he had slept in into a fresh forest green tunic, and fixed his kopis about his waist before splashing his face with some cold water that sat in a bowl on the table. He moved outside and breathed in the morning air. It was crisp and clean.

"Did you sleep well?" Korinna said as she pressed a hand to his smooth cheek.

"I did, I think." He offered a small smile as she took his hand in hers.

"You look different somehow," Korinna said, "suddenly, you seem grown. I want you to have something…" She handed him a bone-handled dagger inlaid with bronze.

"This is too much!" Nicos protested as he turned the weapon over in his hands, marvelling at its beauty.

"It isn't. It has been passed down in my family for longer than I have known, and I never thought I would have a child." She held up her hand to stop Nicos interrupting, "But here you are, and I want you to carry it and let it protect you as it has done me." Korinna kissed his cheek, then fixed the dagger to his belt on the opposite side from the kopis.

"Thank you." It was all Nicos could think to say, but it didn't seem enough.

"Now come, it is time to send you on your way."

They walked with arms linked towards the raised platform at the centre of the settlement. It caught Nicos by surprise to find the whole tribe gathered as they rounded the corner. Hunters lined either side of him as Korinna let go of his arm and went to take her place amongst the other women. Nicos walked forward. Each of the hunters, every woman who had been pivotal in raising him, the women he called family, touched his shoulder. It took all his concentration to keep his emotions under control until he finally reached Thea at the top of the platform. She pulled him into a tight embrace, then turned to face everyone.

"So, it has finally come —the day we say goodbye to our son, Nicos." Thea spoke as only a leader could; her voice steady, but underneath it was a well of sadness that rooted her words. "It has been our honour to raise you in the way of the hunt, and you will always be the son of the hunters. We present to you a gift that will aid you through all that is to come." Thea presented Nicos with a new double-convex bow. It was made with the wood of a yew tree. The ends had been dipped in silver, with the symbol of Artemis carved into it. It was exquisite. Nicos held it firmly in his hand and thanked Thea before turning to face the gathered women.

"How do I thank you? I don't even know how to begin to find the words. You have given me everything, and I will carry you with me in all that I do. To leave you... my home...

is harder than I ever thought. I may not be able to tell anyone who I really am or where I come from, but I will never forget. I am all of you, and I am proud to be your son."

In response, each of the hunters raised their bows above their head in a salute and let out a battle cry, a cry so loud that birds took off from the trees and the horses in the paddock reared up and whinnied. Thea escorted Nicos down from the podium and over to Theron, who stood saddled and ready. He patted his loyal steed on the neck; a sense of relief rippled through him, knowing he would be taking at least one friend with him.

He fixed his new bow over his shoulder and knocked the quiver of arrows into place on the horse, and then he turned to say the goodbye he was dreading most. Nicos looked at Thea and Korinna, took a sharp breath, and pulled them into an embrace. An embrace that spoke of all the things he didn't have the words for. It spoke of the love he held for these two women, who had taught him more than the way of the hunt. They had taught him of love, family, and trust. It spoke of admiration. More than this, it spoke of how he could never and would never forget them.

"To get to Chiron will take you a full week's ride. He will be found on Mount Pelion," Thea said. "Head to Athens first, it's a straight road from the edge of the forest. There you will find Hermia; she will give you a place to rest for the night and food for the journey. It is important you speak to no one in Athens. You understand?"

Nicos nodded his head.

"I mean it. You will find Hermia in the Agora," Thea insisted and handed him the scroll Artemis had given them.

"The Agora. Got it."

"Well, you best be on your way," Korinna said in a quiet voice.

Nicos again nodded and then pulled himself gracefully up on to Theron's back. He looked down at his mothers and smiled at them.

"I love you both. So very much."

With a thought, Theron reared up on his back legs before galloping out of the village. He couldn't look back. He could feel all the eyes of the hunters watching him disappear into the trees. He didn't slow down until Theron came onto the main road headed to Athens.

The afternoon sun was at its peak in the clear blue sky as Nicos reached the entrance into the city. The heat pricked his skin, and Theron's flank was damp with sweat. They slowly strode deeper into the city, his eyes feasting on all the new sights. He was in awe of the city. It was so alive. Alive with sound. The sound of human beings living. Shouts of angry spouses, the yells of merchants. A small child swiped something to eat from a fruit seller and darted off like a rat into the crowds.

Nicos was somewhat spellbound at first at all the different shapes and sizes of each person he passed. The hunters didn't all look identical, of course, but they all had a similar slender, muscled shape. Here the women varied from thin, willowy wisps that might be blown away if Boreas blew too hard to a squat, portly woman that seemed to be blessed with some type of wealth. Then there were the men. Nicos struggled to pull his focus from them at times.

He hadn't known the company of men, not properly. The only experience being men of villages he may have aided, but then he didn't speak to them, nor really did he look at them.

Here in Athens, his eyes danced around at the variety. Sure, he thought women beautiful, but something new stirred in him at the sight of each new male form.

Nicos turned into the main market space that sprawled before the Agora proper, where he found a stable to leave Theron. Nicos instructed a muddy-faced youth to make sure Theron was watered, fed, and brushed down, and threw him a few drachmae. He pulled the quiver arrows from the horse, fixed it over his shoulder, and began to meander through the crowd in search of Hermia.

Instinct kicked in as he felt the stares of passing locals lingering on him. He didn't think he looked anything special, but he had faced enough predators to know when the look was less then friendly. They were mistrustful. Further into the crowded market, he went. Stalls and merchants selling their goods seemed never-ending. The colours that struck him from every corner dazzled his eyes: spices of orange, red, yellow, and brown; fabrics of rich purples, blues, and pink. Then the noise came —screams of haggling and sales pitches, livestock mooing and squealing. Nicos stood still for a moment and, using his keen sight, found a path to some steps leading up to a temple.

There.

Nicos looked like he was performing some intricate dance as he moved through the gathered people of the market. He was silent, quick, and beautiful. A nearby group of Athenians watched in fascination at this feline feat of human movement. He reached the steps and sat, noticing the watchful eyes of the group. Only when they realised that he was now staring back at them did they disperse and hurry off in scattered directions. The steps were mercifully in the shade of the looming temple behind them, and the coolness of them spread through Nicos' body. Grateful for the reprieve from the heat, he pulled his waterskin up to his lips and drank deeply, feeling the chill flow down his throat, spilling into his chest.

He rummaged in the satchel Korinna had given him to find some figs, his favourite. His teeth tore into the soft flesh of the ripe fruit, its juice spilled down his chin. He was hungrier than he realised. Nicos ate a second fig, and as he swallowed it down, he felt the weight of all that had passed. So much had happened in the last day, so much had been learnt, and so much had been left behind. Sorrow fluttered in his chest. Had he said enough to his mothers? Did they know how much he owed them and how much he loved them?

Find Hermia. I will send a message back with Hermia. Find her, and then we can rest. He thought.

That was all he had to do. Simple. Only it wasn't that simple. Nicos could track an animal for miles in forests and wilderness, but finding one person amongst the throng of Athenians was proving to be much harder. A flock of hoopoes flew over the brilliant blue of the sky, their brown feathers turned to warm sand under the light of the sun. An idea. He felt stupid for not thinking of it sooner. His eyes changed from his calm, rich hazel, flecked with green and gold, to that of one of the birds overhead. It dived out of formation and swept over the people below, scanning every face.

Where are you? Where are... YES!

Hermia stood in the shadow of a pillar at the temple. Her eyes caught sight of the strange movement of the bird, it hovered before her, inspecting her, and then, as though breaking a trance, flew back up into the sky and off into the distance. Nicos let out a little chuckle at the look on Hermia's face as he pulled himself up and climbed the stairs. He reached the entrance to the temple and took in its great beauty. Huge marble pillars reached up to support a great marble roof, and inside, he could see candles surrounding a large bronze statue of Hephaestus. Nicos watched an old-bearded man covered in soot and burns lay a hammer at the foot of the statue. A blacksmith, he thought, asking for the god to give him strength in the work he had received.

A small but strong hand clasped his elbow and pulled him from his gaze and down the outside of the temple.

"How lovely to see you too, Hermia." Nicos said as he pulled his elbow free.

"What the hell were you doing with that bird?" Hermia scolded as she stopped in front of him. Her blonde hair was neatly arranged in a plait, and she wore the official garb of the hunters. Forest green robes with bow and arrows fixed at her back; the brown sandals laced up to her knee. She looked around to check they were out of sight and earshot of most people before continuing, "Find me, that was all you had to do! People have noticed you."

"What?" Nicos was genuinely shocked.

"I have heard tell of a light-footed stranger that moves like a nymph. A man dressed as a hunter of Artemis… but you are not to blame. Really, Thea should have thought better than to send you out in this…" She gestured to his forest green attire.

"It's all I had." Nicos stammered.

"I shall fix that before you leave tomorrow. You have to be more cautious, Nicos." Hermia tried to temper the frustration in her voice.

"I will. I'm sorry."

She patted his arm affectionately. "I am just glad you are here. I have a friend who will put you up for the night. Come follow me, you must be starving."

Nicos nodded and followed closely behind Hermia. It was clear she knew Athens as though she had lived here her whole life; perhaps she had. When someone was accepted into the hunters, the need to know of their life prior seemed unimportant. Hermia navigated them down one back street after another, always able to find the route with the least amount of people. They talked little as they manoeuvred the streets.

"Wait here a moment." Hermia said.

She crossed a street and disappeared inside a grand-looking house. Nicos leant back against the wall and waited. It wasn't long until he heard the familiar whistle that was used to call a hunter's attention. He looked across the way to see Hermia just inside the doorway. Nicos stepped out to cross the street, only to collide heavily into someone; the force of it knocked him to the ground.

"I'm so sorry!" Nicos said looking up at the man before him. He was tall and broad, with smooth, tousled brown hair. A knee-length grey chiton draped over him, although it barely concealed his hair-covered chest. Nicos noticed three scars cut over his left pectoral, and the broach of an owl was fixed over his right. A well-kept beard covered his handsome face. What struck Nicos the most was the man's smile; it was dazzling. It lit up his face. He had never seen anything so beautiful.

"Umm, no, don't be, it's my fault," a deep voice responded. "Here," he offered a hand to Nicos, which he took and was pulled upright again. "Are you alright?"

"Yes, fine thank you." Nicos smiled in response as he dusted himself off.

The two of them stared at each other. Nicos was about to ask his name but was cut off by a sharp whistle.

Hermia.

"Sorry again." Nicos blurted out as he carried on towards the house. As he reached the door, he glanced back over his shoulder and smiled to see the handsome stranger watching him still as he disappeared inside the house.

"What was that?" Hermia asked as soon as the door closed behind them.

"Nothing. I just wasn't looking where I was going." Nicos replied.

Hermia wrinkled her brow. "Right, well, this is Jocasta. She will give you a room for the night. I am going to fetch Theron and pick up some things for your journey. Please stay out of sight and attract no attention. The rumours of the male hunter of Artemis are becoming louder and louder."

Nicos nodded his head.

Jocasta was a striking woman. Not in beauty, although it could be argued she was beautiful in her youth. No, she was striking because of her fierceness. Her face was sharp and angular, as though if you were to touch it, you would cut yourself. She was thin, and her hair was greying. Nicos followed her through the open space of the ground floor. It was littered with cushions of red, orange, and fur. A thick, perfumed scent hung in the air. It was intoxicating. He followed her upstairs and down a hallway that looked down into the cushioned space below. Jocasta opened a door with a rusty key at the very end.

"This is for you then," she said with a raspy, hard-edged voice. "Working hours begin at sundown, so be sure to stay out of sight." Jocasta handed him the key before turning and leaving him alone.

The room was simple. It had a bed against one wall with pillow and sheets. There was a table set with a plain goblet, a jug of wine, bread and olives, and some fruit. A window looked out over part of Athens; it really was quite beautiful. Nicos noticed the stable was directly below, which gave him comfort knowing Theron would be close by tonight. A bronze bowl of water sat atop a small table in front of the window, and a fresh cloth hung from the side of the bowl. Nicos sat on the edge of the bed and pulled off his sandals, flexing his feet in relief. As he did, a sigh escaped his mouth. He moved over to the bowl of water, he pulled off his forest green tunic and discarded it to the floor before reaching his hands up above his head and stretching the tight muscles of his body.

The late afternoon sun spilled like liquid amber over the streets and rooftops outside. Some of it found its way into his room and onto his torso as he picked up the cloth and soaked it in the cool water. What he wouldn't give to be able to dip into the stream that ran alongside the hunters village; still, the damp cloth was soothing and refreshing against his warm skin.

Nicos started with his face before moving lower, careful to get every inch of his body. The clear water that had filled the bronze bowl had slowly turned murky; it had surprised him to see how dirty the day had made him. Lastly, he lifted the bowl out of its stand and set it on the floor at the foot of the bed. He sat down, lowering his feet into the water. His toes danced in the liquid, making small ripples.

After a little time had passed, he dried off his feet, enjoying that they had returned again to their soft pink colour instead of the dusty grey they had been before he soaked them. Nicos picked up the bowl of dirty water and emptied it out of the window, making sure, of course, that no one was below. He then returned it to where it had been when he had first entered the room. He patted his flat stomach as it gave a little rumble. The plate of bread and olives didn't last long and was washed down with a healthy cup or two of the sweet red wine. Again, he sat on the bed, enjoying the late afternoon breeze that found its way through his window, kissing his bare skin. Nicos lay back and, without meaning to, fell asleep.

9

Helios, on his great chariot, pulled the sun out of sight as Selene took her place. A great full moon floated amongst the shimmering constellations on a blanket of dark royal blue sky. The air still held the heat of the day, though a noticeable chill had crept in. It prickled the naked body of Nicos, causing him to stir slowly from his slumber. How long had he been asleep? He moved over to the window and smiled to see Theron in the stable.

Good to see you, my friend.

Theron looked up to the window as though Nicos had spoken the words out loud and answered him with a pleasing huff before returning to munching on the hay at his feet. A small shiver rippled through Nicos. He turned to pick up his tunic from the floor, only to find it neatly folded on top of the table. Next to it was a burgundy chiton. He moved over to them and found a note placed on top of the burgundy.

Nicos,

Please wear the burgundy. I didn't want to wake you, as you looked so peaceful. Theron is in the stable and has been well fed. See you at dawn.

Hermia.

He pulled on the new clothes; the fabric was soft against his skin. It occurred to him that he had never worn anything that wasn't fashioned and made by hunters before. It was much more comfortable. Nicos thought to fill his bronze bowl with fresh water if he was to leave so early tomorrow, so he picked up a clay jug and headed for the door. He stepped out into the hallway to hear a cacophony of voices and laughter coming from behind other doors and from the space below. Jocasta's voice whispered in his memory, *Work hours begin at sundown.*

He hesitated for a moment, wondering whether fetching the water was a good idea or not. He decided it was. That, and his curiosity peaked. Slowly and silently, Nicos continued further down the hallway and looked over the banister. A group of musicians played music that teased some of the gathered people to dance. Others lounged on the cushions with a young woman or man draped over them. There were some that wore chiffon that covered little, leaving nothing to the imagination.

The others were in varying stages of undress, though their clothes seemed to be that of everyday attire. Nicos spotted a group of young men in military uniform, but the way they were drinking and heckling made it clear they were not on duty. He moved down the stairs, trying to look like he wasn't out of place amongst all the frivolity and debauchery. There was no mistaking the business Jocasta was running. A smirk seemed fixed on Nicos' face. He made it outside to the well and pulled up some fresh water. As he decanted it from the bucket into his jug, the back of his neck prickled. He was being watched.

Cautiously, he picked up the heavy jug and turned to head back into the house. His eyes were sharp and keen, seeking out who was watching him.

Where are you?

It was impossible to see anyone staring directly at him. In truth, everyone was looking at everyone, or they were fixated on the company they were with. Shaking off the feeling, Nicos made his way quickly back up the stairs, knocked out of the way on the top step as two of the soldiers he spied earlier sprinted past with a giggling woman who was already completely naked. Nicos couldn't help himself from letting out a small laugh. Just as he reached his door, the sensation of being watched came over him again. He slipped inside his room and closed the door. As fast as he could, he put the jug down, grabbed the key off the table and went to lock the door. Just as the key was about to slide into the lock, a knock came.

"I know you are in there." A voice said.

Nicos was calming his breath. You must never let anyone see you are afraid, then they will think you are prey. He was not prey. Not to anyone. The person knocked again.

"I think you have the wrong room." Nicos replied in as firm a tone as he could muster.

"I haven't. I have been looking for you since I got here."

There was something in the disembodied voice that had a hint of familiarity.

"Hang on a moment." Nicos said. He quickly decided to hide anything that might show he was affiliated with the hunters. He pushed his kopis, bow, and arrows under the bed, picking up the dagger and holding it firmly in his hand behind his back.

Let's see who you are, then.

Nicos opened the door. "You!"

"Me." The handsome face of the stranger he had collided with beamed at him. He was in the same clothes he had been wearing when they met, and he clutched an empty goblet in his hand.

"Do you want to come in?" Nicos offered as he stepped aside to allow the man to enter his room. Nicos looked down the hallway to see if anyone else was watching and then closed the door firmly.

"I didn't know if you would remember me." The stranger smiled. "Though it seems you do."

Nicos put the dagger down on the table. The handsome stranger watched him with a mix of surprise and amusement.

"Are you drunk?" Nicos smirked.

"Not drunk, but definitely past sober." He poured himself some wine from the jug on the table, pouring one for Nicos too, before handing him the goblet. "Join me for one?"

"Why were you looking for me?" Nicos took the goblet but did not drink. This man was every bit as handsome as he remembered.

"Hmm? Oh well… I… erm… wanted to make sure you were alright."

"That's all?" Nicos laughed.

He laughed too; it was rich and warm. "Also, when I saw you come into Jocasta's place, I was curious. It's not often she gets new… talent."

Nicos flushed in embarrassment, "Oh no, I don't work here. I am just boarding for the night."

"Shame." He winked, moving towards Nicos. Nicos could feel the heat of him as he put just a few inches between them.

His eyes darted from the man's mischievous green eyes to his full lips. "You are quite beautiful! Do you have a name?"

"Y…yes. I am Nicos." Nicos' voice was soft.

He closed more of the very little distance between them. Nicos could feel his breath on his face. His eyes began to close as he leant up towards the others mouth when suddenly a loud crash and harsh voice shattered the moment.

"What in the name of Hades are you doing? Out! NOW!" Jocasta had burst through the door in a rage. Not a loud, angry rage, but one that you knew not to answer back to. "I don't want to see you in my home again tonight, Zander!" She slapped the back of his legs, making him wince, and let out a yelp as he hurried from the room. Nicos started to follow, but Jocasta slammed the door closed and turned to face him. "You are supposed to be staying out of sight, you idiot boy."

"Jocasta I'm sorry. I had met him earlier today…" Nicos reply was weak and sounded pathetic.

"I don't care! You don't know who he is at all. I have been charged to look after you for a night, and I will not be put at risk!" Jocasta snatched the key that still sat in the lock. "I don't know much of who you are, but I know that you are protected by Artemis and Apollo. Zander is the descendant of one of the oldest families in Athens, making him an ally of Athena… If he were to learn anything about you, then gods help us."

"I only told him my name," Nicos said.

"Let's hope that isn't too much." Jocasta was gone before Nicos could say anything else, and he heard the click of the lock. She had locked him in. It seemed futile to fight it. Perhaps she was right anyway; at least now he would be forced to keep out of trouble. Nicos flopped down on the bed, annoyed and frustrated. He had to be more careful; he knew that. However, he couldn't say he was upset at having been so close to Zander.

10

The clouds roiled above the palace of Olympus in anger. The dark grey clouds shadowed the land below, and cracks of electric blue lightning fractured the air, threatening to unleash an Olympian rage on the Grecian world below. Hera and Ares stood side by side, watching the furious Zeus as he held Apollo by the throat, his feet dangling above the marble floor.

"Tell me why, you insolent bastard!" Zeus roared into the young gods face. Apollo choked on a response. In a thunderous roar of frustration, Zeus flung the God of Light across the pantheon, sending him crashing into the back of a throne. Demeter made to help him only for Zeus to order her to stay where she was. Demeter looked at Apollo spluttering on the floor, her eyes filled with a longing to help. Hera and Ares stood watching Zeus pace back and forth, thunder rumbling above them. Artemis stepped into being behind her brother and was instantly by his side.

"Leave him!" Zeus said in a tone of supreme authority. Artemis looked at her father with venom.

"I will not!" She retorted and took Apollo's face in her hands.

Hera grabbed her husband by the arm, in which he had begun to raise a thunderbolt. She whispered something to him that tempered him slightly, but it was enough. He lowered the bolt, his expression still furious. Demeter saw her opportunity to aid the twins. Ares sat on his throne and let out a satisfied laugh. Apollo had been helped to his feet by his sister and Demeter. His cuts and bruises were slowly starting to heal. They took longer when afflicted by another divine being, longer still when the divine being was the supreme king.

Zeus was in hushed council with Hera, throwing seething looks in the direction of Apollo. He pushed himself away from Demeter and Artemis and went to the far edge of the palace, finding the rays of sunlight to bask in and aid his recovery. His slender fingers ran along his throat, where he could still feel the impression of Zeus' fat fingers.

"What the hell happened?" Artemis asked Demeter quietly.

Demeter looked over to see if anyone, mainly Zeus, was listening before saying, "Apollo refused to tell why he silenced his Oracle in Delphi."

"Why should that matter?" Artemis' heart skipped in her chest. "Have we not all taken out our whim on a mortal before?"

"It seems this Oracle spoke of a vision that we were part of. You know, ever since the incident with the Titan witch of Aeaea, Zeus has kept a close ear to the mortal realm, particularly those gifted with sight, for any mention of us and anything that could threaten us." Demeter was talking softly now, with worry tangled in every word.

"What do you think?" Artemis asked.

"I think... the world is changing. Olympus too. Zeus' paranoia makes me wonder. I have never seen him so at odds... not since Prometheus."

Artemis placed a soothing hand on Demeter's arm and kissed her cheek. She then moved over to her brother, only to be met by Athena in her flowing white dress, her signature plumed helmet held under her arm. Artemis hadn't seen her arrive.

"Sister," Athena greeted formally.

"Athena." Artemis offered an equally formal reply. Athena stalked past her towards her father, placing her helmet down on her seat as she passed it. Artemis reached her brother, placed a hand on his shoulder, and sighed in relief to see that he was almost fully healed. They could not risk speaking out loud, instead, they spoke to each other with their minds, a gift they had mastered in the early hours of their existence.

What were you thinking?

I wasn't. Word was spreading, so I pulled her tongue from her mouth to silence it.

Mortals saw you?

Yes. I was rash but, I was protecting the boy.

And Zeus?

He wants to know what was said.

Then lie!

He will know!

A cough broke their focus, and they turned in perfect unison to see that those who were there had taken to their respective thrones. They moved silently to their seats and sat masking any emotion from their faces.

"So, it seems, brother Apollo," Athena stood as she addressed the circle, "that you have caused quite the upset. Tell me, dear brother, why won't you answer the Sky Father? What are you hiding?"

"I am hiding nothing!" Apollo responded in a calm, steady voice. "It has never been a concern before when we have dealt with false prophets… I mean, did you not blind and torture a mortal man with harpies?"

Zeus lurched forward towards his son, only to be stopped by Athena stepping between them and raising a hand to her father. Zeus stayed himself like a trained dog at Athena's gesture, instead, a great echo of thunder rolled above them, ricocheting around the hall.

"That is true. However, when questioned about things as trivial as you are implying, we have all answered, so why don't you?" Athena was steady and firm.

Apollo huffed, "I remember a time when we all could do as we please. Our business was our own. The Delphic Oracle was speaking false visions. The Oracle receives their visions from me, and I have not seen these visions she proclaimed, so I took her tongue."

"Tell us then if it is so false. Put this argument to rest!" It was Demeter that spoke, her voice soothing all in her motherly way. Apollo looked to Artemis; she, however, had her eyes locked on Athena. Apollo followed her gaze and saw it too. The bright glint in Athena's grey eyes. She had some trick up her sleeve. They had come to know this look. Over the ages, they had seen it appear —Artemis first, right before she had an idea or revealed some plan that would shake up anything. As if on cue, Athena grinned, waving her hand over the mirror world. The smooth surface rippled as if a small stone had fallen into its centre. As it calmed, it showed a clear view into the centre of Delphi, where a beggar woman held out her hands for drachmae, but everyone avoided her. Some even lobbed stones. When she would open her mouth to protest, only a garbled noise left it. The woman had no tongue. The Oracle of Delphi.

"Is this not your once-great Oracle, Apollo?" Athena cooed.

Apollo swallowed hard.

"Bring her to us. Now." Athena commanded, though in truth it was more of a threat.

Apollo stood; his eyes locked on Athena; behind her, he could see Zeus smiling in early triumph. He vanished from the pantheon and appeared before the Oracle. The gods watched from their palace. They watched as she cowered, begging for mercy before Apollo. This made Ares howl with laughter, and Hera too couldn't fight a smirk. Artemis watched her brother and saw beyond the fear of the woman. Instead, she saw how her brother gently offered his hand to the distraught beggar. She could hear the harmonious tone of his voice interlaced with pity and regret. Demeter too could see his compassion, always admiring anyone who offered grace to others. The great reflection of the world sank into the marble floor, and in the centre of the throne circle stood Apollo and the Oracle.

A scream, or at least what Artemis and Demeter assumed was a scream, escaped the Oracle as she flung herself on the ground before them all. Her arms outstretched as her forehead touched the floor, and garbled noises littered the air.

"Look to me, mortal," Zeus commanded. Athena stood to his right, her plumed helmet now atop her head. The Oracle obeyed, squinting her eyes as the divine beauty of the Sky Father burnt her a little. "Do you remember your last vision before Apollo cruelly took your tongue?"

The terrified woman nodded.

"Apollo, you will return this mortal's tongue to her. For though you are the god of prophecy, I will judge its validity," Zeus said with great satisfaction.

Apollo looked as though he might refuse. How could he though in front of those assembled? He knelt and turned the Oracle to face him. She trembled at his touch.

"Open your mouth," Apollo instructed.

The Oracle closed her eyes in shame and fear as she did as the god asked. Apollo reached his thumb and index finger inside her mouth and pinched at the nub of tongue root left. Slowly, he pulled it forward as a fresh, fleshy tongue began to form. It was agony for the Oracle. In fact, she didn't know what had been worse —having her tongue torn out or having a new one regrown. Ares again laughed with wicked enjoyment at the suffering before him.

Hera chided him, though it did little to stop his laughing as he watched the hands of the Oracle grip into her thighs, so tightly that she drew blood. Moved by her bravery and perhaps more at her own guilt, as she knew it was no fault of the Oracle, only she had seen something that must not be shared, not if Nicos was to stay safe and hidden as long as he could. Artemis glided to her side and took one hand in her own. Demeter followed and took her other hand. They offered the glow of their divinity to sooth the pain, even if it was only a little. Athena cocked her head to one side at the sight of this. It was odd, she thought.

With a final primal scream, the job was done. The Oracle of Delphi was whole again. Apollo touched her lightly under her chin, just on the softest part, and her pain was gone.

"Tell me of your last prophetic vision, great Oracle of Delphi!" Zeus said impatiently.

It was in this moment that the poor Oracle became fully aware again of her surroundings. The pain of regrowing her tongue had blinded her from seeing Artemis and Demeter at her side holding her hands, which they still did now. She nodded in thanks as they helped her to her feet before returning to their respective places in the circle. Apollo then bowed to her and made his way to sit. The floor was hers. With a deep breath, she began.

"My visions, gifted to me by the great Apollo, have always come clear and sure to me, mighty Zeus. I never told a false prophecy before…" The Oracles voice was sure, but it had a tremor of nerves under it. "This vision was different, but I know it wasn't false. It came to me broken and clouded. My visions have always been clear as water, but this… it filled me with unease and fear."

"I don't care how you felt about it; all I want to know is what you bloody saw! Do you want me to take your tongue again for wasting my time?" thundered Zeus.

The Oracle held up her hands as though they might shield her from Zeus' attack. "I will tell you, but it makes little sense. I saw a child twice blessed. A war between the Olympians and then… nothing."

Zeus was on his feet, quick as lightning, and had lifted the Oracle by her shoulders into the air. "What do you mean by nothing? Who is this child? What comes of a war between gods? ANSWER ME!!!"

"I don't know my lord." The Oracle whimpered; her new tongue suddenly felt fat in her mouth. "I see the beginning of the war but not its cause; it's as though it is covered in smoke. The child, I see its place of birth, but then it fades as quickly as it comes. When I try to focus in on the child, I see glimpses of people and places. A village in a forest, a mountain, a city, but then it goes as though it is outside of fate itself. I cannot see beyond it. I promise you; this is all I see." Tears streamed down the Oracle's face. Artemis and Apollo stole a glance at each other.

"Where was the child born?" asked Hera as she stepped up next to her husband.

"The island of the witch," she sobbed.

"Circe." Ares said coldly as he too stood up, paying closer attention now than he had. Zeus roared, and lightning rippled through his body, causing the Oracle between his hands to scream and smoke as it coursed through her. She jerked in his arms as she burnt from the inside out. Zeus dropped the lifeless corpse to the floor. It landed with a dull thud, her eyes and mouth wide open in fear. Artemis noticed the still bright pink tongue that Apollo had gifted, fresh and unharmed in her mouth.

"That deceitful bitch had a child?" Zeus boomed. No other god dared to speak. The revelations from the Oracle unsettled them all. "How you didn't think to share any of this Apollo is beyond my understanding!"

"Her vision was broken," Apollo retorted.

Athena whispered into Zeus' ear. His eyes widened at whatever she was saying. All the gathered divine beings felt something shift in the air, an uneasiness was rippling through them all.

"Come before us, Moirai," Zeus spoke into the sky.

The air stood thick and still. Ares, Hera, and Athena moved to stand beside Zeus. Demeter joined the twins as, in the centre of the pantheon, appeared the Fates.

"Hail Zeus." The three Moirai greeted in perfect union. Lakhesis bowed her head, as did her sisters Klotho and Atropos.

"To what do we owe the honour of being called before you?" Klotho asked.

"Do not play coy with me. You who see all our destinies are summoned before me, as you knew you would be, to answer a question." Zeus answered.

"We reveal the future to no one." Lakhesis scolded.

"YOU WILL TO ME!" thundered Zeus.

Atropos placed her hand on Lakhesis' arm as she stepped forward towards the Olympian king. "We will answer only one question; it is all we can offer." Her voice was soothing but firm.

"I want…" Zeus began before Athena interrupted.

"Father, might I ask the question?"

Zeus nodded in agreement. Athena stepped before the Fates and bowed respectfully.

"Great Moirai, we have heard of a war and a child; I believe they are interlinked. How?"

The sisters turned to each other. Atropos lifted their shared eye to the sky and let it hover above them. It began to grow bigger above them until it was the size of a small boulder, floating lazily as it shimmered in its ocean green glory. Slowly, shapes began to form and fade into being. All that was said next was spoken in harmonious unison by the Fates.

"We are the Moirai, and we see all. The fates of living beasts, mortal and divine. We see your birth, your life, and your death. For death comes to all things. A child was born of the great witch, Circe, a child outside of fate. When it touches the life of another, we lose sight of that being's life however, long they are together. Changing their destiny from the one once woven. A war is coming to Olympus, but its outcome is unknown."

The glowing orb showed mortals of no importance to the gods watching. Shapes of buildings appeared and disappeared. The shadow of a centaur flashed up and was gone in the blink of an eye. Artemis chanced a look at Apollo. He saw it too.

Who else? She thought.

Athena surely had; she rarely missed anything, but upon looking at her, she noticed that Athena was staring at a temple with a sly grin on her face. Klotho, Lakhesis, and Atropos turned to face Zeus once more.

"Who fathered this child?" Zeus' voice was just above a whisper and filled with such hatred that it chilled the bones of Artemis and Apollo.

"We gave you one question, and that is all." Lakhesis answered.

"Do not ask us anymore, Zeus," Atropos warned as she teased a thick golden thread from her robe. Zeus' own fate. If it was her will, she could end it now. An empty threat as the three Fates believed too heavily in the grand design of the universe, but Zeus would not take that risk. With that they were gone.

"I want this child found!" Zeus ordered, "Do whatever you must, but find it and bring it to me! Surely it means to destroy us as its mother tried."

"What if it means to save us?" It was the gentle voice of Demeter that asked. Artemis and Apollo looked over to their fellow Olympian. Could she be an ally in what was to come?

Zeus thundered in response, "Demeter, this is a child of Circe; it will bear no goodwill to us." As he finished, the gods who hadn't been present were within the palace. Aphrodite, Poseidon, Dionysus, Hermes, and Hephaestus.

"My fellow Olympians," Zeus addressed them all with superiority, a voice that demanded obedience, "there is a child that must be found. It is a child of Circe, and it means to do us harm. Find it. Also, I want you all to heed this decree… No more will you fornicate with mortals. Any bastard children you have on earth will be declared to me."

The looks of shock and indignation varied around the circle of thrones. Apollo and Artemis' faces were masks of stone showing nothing. Their only concern was making sure Nicos made it to Chiron. There were minor objections that fell on deaf ears. No one answered Aphrodite when she asked who was the owner of the charred corpse that still adorned the floor.

"Do you have an idea of where to start looking for this child?" Dionysus asked as he glugged down some wine.

"Artemis will accompany me to her hunters near Attica, as it seems a likely place to begin with what our old Oracle of Delphi shared," Zeus gestured to the still smouldering body. Aphrodite seemed pleased at last to know who it was.

"I can go alone, dear father," Artemis said calmly.

"No. We shall go together, my daughter. I must make sure you aren't as deceitful as your brother," Zeus replied. Artemis gave a slight nod of her head in acceptance.

"I will go to Athens. I noticed the temple of Hephaestus for a moment in what the Fates have shared. I have loyal servants there who can keep an eye out for me. I suggest you all go to any allies you have in Greece and set your spies,"

Athena said, and then was gone. Quickly, the others followed, heading to their favoured cities and followers. Apollo and Artemis were left alone, facing Zeus.

"Don't you want to get going too, my dear twins?" Zeus asked dangerously.

"Yes, of course father." They answered.

11

Nicos awoke to the click of the bedroom door being unlocked. He lay still, his hand reaching under his pillow, delicate fingers wrapping around the dagger that lay concealed there. A scent of fresh forest filled his nostrils, and he released his grip on the weapon and sat up. Hermia greeted him as she began to collect up his things, sorting it into two piles.

"Good morning," Nicos' voice was still filled with sleep. "What are you doing?" He rubbed his eyes and stretched. Out the window, he could see the first light of dawn and the sky the colour of peach.

"This is what you can take." Hermia pointed to a new satchel of rough-worn leather, his kopis, bow, and arrow. His hunters' garments sat folded in another pile with his old satchel. "I will return this to our tribe. Before you start, there are too many eyes looking for a male hunter now, and we cannot risk you being tied to us. For your sake, get up and get ready; you need leave in the next hour before Helios has the sun completely above the horizon." She turned and left the room.

Nicos pulled himself up out of the bed, and washed in the bronze bowl, drank some goats milk that Hermia had placed next to a plate of bread and cheese. He didn't dawdle in getting dressed and pulling on his sandals. What was the point? He had to leave, and the sooner he was on his way, the sooner he would reach Chiron. The sooner he might have more answers to what was expected of him. Inspecting his new, though clearly pre-owned, satchel, he saw it was filled with some food as well as some small jars of concoctions he knew must have come from Korinna. One for burns, one to aid sleep, and one to help you see in the dark. Even now, they watched out for him. He fixed his belt around the burgundy chiton, attaching the dagger of Korinna, and slung his bow over his shoulder; the arrows must have been taken by Hermia already.

Nicos made his way downstairs, seeing the remnants of the night before: spilled wine, pieces of clothing, and half-eaten food. Just before he reached the door that led out to the stable, Jocasta called out. He turned to see her crossing towards him.

"Be smart out there. Remember, you are your own person, not some plaything of gods." Jocasta whispered, as though someone might hear. She pulled a silver hair pin from her hair and turned Nicos around to tie up his own hair whilst fixing the pin in place. "Beautiful and deadly. It is as sharp as the fang of a serpent. Just in case."

She linked his arm to escort him the rest of the way to the stable. Hermia stood beside Theron, who looked like polished obsidian in the early dawn light. Nicos flung his arms around Hermia and held her so tightly. This would be the last hunter he would see for a long time, if not ever again. They embraced for a long minute.

"Give this to Thea for me." Nicos handed her a letter, rolled tightly, and bound with a piece of green material torn from his old tunic. Hermia smiled and tucked the parchment into her own satchel. With nothing left to say, Nicos pulled himself up onto Theron's back. Jocasta and Hermia stood side by side, watching him leave.

The streets were so quiet. It almost felt like a brand-new Athens in comparison to what it had been like when he arrived yesterday. There was the odd merchant setting up their goods, and here and there, a beggar was sleeping. Theron's hoofs fell nearly silent on the stones as they made their way. Above them, the sky was getting a little brighter, its peach colour changing now to a pale yellow. Coming towards them was another horse with a man astride it. Nicos couldn't stop the smile that broke across his face. Zander —that's what Jocasta had called him. He too smiled at the sight of Nicos as he pulled his dapple-grey horse to a halt.

"Good morning to you, Nicos." His voice was like honey.

"Zander… How's your head?" Nicos asked.

"Ha, it is fine, a little heavy perhaps. I must apologise if I made a fool of myself last night." His sincerity touched Nicos. "Are you leaving Athens so soon?"

"I am. Though I hope to return one day," Nicos said, making Zander blush slightly. Nicos noticed the pin on Zander's tunic, a silver owl. He had clocked it when they first met, but he was sure its eyes didn't glow like that before. "A curious pin," Nicos remarked.

Something flashed across Zander's face as he looked down at the pin.

"It's a family heirloom. I wish I could stay and chat, but I have to go. I hope I see you again, Nicos." Zander shouted as he charged his horse forward. Nicos watched him gallop off through the streets and out of sight.

Strange. Still, on we go, Theron, we have much ground to cover.

***

Zander rode as fast as he could through the streets of Athens as they began to fill with waking Athenians. The eyes on his owl broach glowed brightly, and the heat was starting to burn the skin beneath it. He had been given the broach when he was just eight-years-old —a day burnt into his memory. His father, Zenon, was a devout member and leader in the Parliament of Athena. It was an ancient group completely dedicated to the grey-eyed goddess.

Zenon had told the young Zander that they were descended from the first families that settled Athens and aided Athena in her war with Poseidon to decide who would win the newly founded city. In return, she gifted the six families that fought alongside her a broach of pure silver, forged in the fires of Hephaestus, and they formed the first Parliament. It was decreed then that all first-born children would be inducted into the order. Zenon took his son to the temple of Athena and instructed him to go inside and wait. Zander stepped into the vast interior and approached the statue of the goddess. Hanging bowls of beaten gold were ablaze, lining the walls and casting a soft glow about the place.

"Welcome Zander, son of Zenon," Athena's voice echoed around the temple. Zander turned around on the spot, seeking the origin of the voice. His heart was in his throat. Out of the air stepped Athena in ethereal splendour, dressed in a white dress and her helmet. Zander dropped to his knees and prostrated before her.

"Arise, boy," she commanded.

Zander scrambled to his feet to look up at the goddess. He gasped at her beauty as his eyes began to sting.

"You are to join the Parliament of Athena; it is your right as the first-born of the next generation. A gift I bestowed in honour of your forebear's service to me. Will you be all that I desire? Will you do what is asked of you? Will you honour and devote yourself to me and only me for all of your short mortal life?" Athena spoke with such authority that the young Zander struggled to keep his body from trembling.

"I do." Zander answered, surprised at the steadiness of his own voice.

"Then welcome, my child." Athena smiled and waved her hand towards Zander. A burning began on the right side of his chest. He wanted to let out a scream but felt the eyes of Athena watching him, daring him to break. He did not. In sharp breaths, he endured the burning for what felt like hours, until just as quickly as it had begun, it stopped. In its place was a silver owl fastened to his tunic.

Athena let out a laugh and clapped her hands together. "Well, I shall keep a close eye on you, Zander. The first in a very long time that did not scream, cry, or piss themselves, like your father. I will see you again."

Zander stood alone in the temple. His knees gave way beneath him, and he fell to the cold marble floor, his breath heaving in his chest. He didn't know how long he stayed there, but it was the first light of dawn when he finally stepped out of the temple to be met with the beaming pride of Zenon.

Now, as Zander reached the temple, he was greeted by five others, all with the same glowing-eyed owls. They greeted each other fondly as they climbed the stairs. One of them, a young woman with dark hair, gave hurried words to a priestess, and within moments she was hurrying out the other priestesses in the temple and swore they would stop anyone from coming in.

All stood silently, only the sound of their breathing could be heard. Just as she had done before, Athena appeared before them in magnificent splendour. Everyone bowed their heads in respect. With a flick of her wrist, six chairs and a throne appeared in a circle. Athena sat, removed her helmet, and gestured for the others to take their place. Zander took his place on her right-hand side.

"I have work of utmost importance for you, my Parliament. I need you to find someone. They will be now in their eighteenth cycle. Be wary of them; we believe they are a being of dangerous power." Athena spoke calmly, though Zander swore he could hear something else in her voice, something like fear, but that would be impossible, he thought. "Keep your eyes sharp for any strangers that come into Athens; the smallest of oddities must be investigated. I have it on great authority that they will be passing this way. This is a threat to Olympus and all of Greece. Find them, bind them, and call for me."

Athena arose and looked at her assembled followers, almost smiled, and turned into the air. The moment she was gone, frantic whispers passed amongst them. It wasn't often Athena called upon them, and when she had, it had been for some war or other. This was bigger; it felt more urgent. Zander began to think now that maybe it was fear, or perhaps worry, that he had heard hiding inside her words.

"What of that youth yesterday? Could he be who we are meant to be looking for?" asked a short, stocky man.

"Who Atreus?" asked Zander.

"I was in the market yesterday with Alexandra," he said, waving his arm in the direction of the dark-haired woman who had been talking to the priestess. "We saw a beautiful youth move through the people like he was made of water, ducking and weaving like a nymph."

Alexandra looked over. "It was odd, Zander. I would have thought no more on it, but now with the charge of Athena, should we look into it further?"

"Perhaps. What did they look like?"

"Lean and of decent height," Alexandra recalled.

"She had rich brown hair and streaks of something like copper running through it." Atreus added.

"She? I thought they were a man… though now you mention it, it could have been a young woman." Alexandra interrupted.

"No, you're right, it was a man. I remember, I think." said Atreus.

Zander turned to hide his face from them all. Could they be talking about Nicos? No, surely not, he thought. Yet that is who they were describing. Nicos couldn't be a threat to anyone. Though he had that dagger ready in his hand last night at Jocasta's.

"It is a good place to start. Take the market, and I will take my own lead. I think I remember seeing someone like this around Jocasta's place. Keep in contact." Zander said as he made his way from the temple. He clambered up on to his horse and made his way back to his family home. It would take him less than an hour to pack up what he needed and be on his way, meaning Nicos would only be an hour or two ahead of him. Perhaps he could catch up and find out if this was the mortal his goddess demanded.

***

The ride towards Mount Pelion was set to take Nicos several days. It made him wince at the thought, as he already felt the slight familiar ache that came with riding for long periods of time. The first few hours of his journey had been quite serene since leaving Athens. He had enjoyed seeing people wake up and start their day, as well as greeting the odd passer-by. Theron seemed to be enjoying the steady pace at which they moved. The sky above them had become quite overcast as the morning progressed, keeping the air cooler than it had been the last few days.

It was early in the evening when Nicos started to think about finding a place to rest for the night. He pulled Theron to a halt and, using his exceptional sight, cast his eyes around to see if he could spot somewhere to stay. Up ahead, he could see, tucked up off the road, a small pond with a cave behind it.

Up there, my friend.

It took no time at all for the pair to reach the pond. Nicos dismounted and pulled off all the gear Theron had been carrying. As soon as the horse was freed, it gave a whinny and small on-the-spot trot of happiness. Nicos smiled to see such unbridled happiness in his friend. As Theron bowed his head to drink, Nicos inspected the mouth of the cave. Bones littered the floor. He paused to look as far as his eyes could see inside the dark void. Something moved inside. Two, maybe three, somethings. As silently as he could, he moved back out towards Theron, picking up one of the bones as he did so.

"Shall we see who's home?" Nicos smirked at Theron.

The horse stood strong just behind him. With a flick of his wrist, the bone clattered into the cave. The sound of growls and soft footfalls grew louder as five large wolves of brown and grey emerged. They all bared their teeth and eyed the delicious-looking intruders. Nicos could sense the increased heart rate of his steed. Theron was nervous, but he stood his ground. Nicos, however, had no fear in him. He instead stepped towards the largest of the wolves.

"I will not hurt you if you will not harm my friend and I." Nicos' voice was calm and soothing. The wolf let out a low growl. "We mean you no harm, sweet friend." His hand reached out as the wolf bowed its head to let Nicos stroke his coarse fur. The others sniffed at Theron, but soon let him be as the alpha snapped at them. They all made their way back inside the darkness of the cave, that is, except the largest one, who settled himself in the mouth of the cave. Protecting his family, just in case.

Nicos gathered some dry twigs and built up a small fire before sitting down, his back resting against the wolf, that had now closed its eyes. Theron, still wary, set himself on the other side of the fire; after all he was a horse, and they were wolves. Nicos looked up into the night sky; it was still cloudy, but he could make out stars every now and then. For the first time, he let himself wonder about the gods themselves. He wondered what they might be doing right now. Were they out looking for him? What might they do if they found him?

Kill me, most likely.

It was a reasonable thought. I mean, isn't that what he was supposed to be learning to do to them? He hadn't really considered the latter part of what he had been told much before now. He was to affect the outcome of a war between the Olympians. Wars were solved with death, submission, or peace, and the latter two didn't seem possible. Chiron would help him get ready; after all, it was Chiron who helped train Achilles, Heracles, and Jason. Then his thoughts drifted to his birth mother as the fire crackled. Circe.

Artemis had spoken her name so lovingly, but Nicos knew so little about her. Yes, he had heard tales of the cruel witch of Aeaea who transformed trespassers on her island but growing up with the hunters he learnt quickly how fast men will twist the tales of great women. He knew how much they feared even the notion of a powerful woman. It was something that always made him chuckle, the people who told of the murderous, primitive hunters of Artemis were the same people who came begging for their help. Nicos decided he would ask Artemis, when he could, to tell him more about Circe. At some point, his eyes grew heavy, and he fell into a dream-filled sleep, the alpha wolf acting as his pillow.

Nicos' dreams usually came clear and enlightened him to some new concoction to create, but this night they were broken into harsh pieces. One moment, he stood at the gates of Hades. The terrifying three-headed Cerberus barked as it raised one of its huge paws to slash at Nicos. Then he stood in a chariot of gold being pulled by two black-scaled dragons. As it plummeted down, he was thrown out of the chariot, his body tumbling towards the ground below. Seconds before he hit the earth, Nicos was standing. Standing on the bones of children, and in the darkness, he could hear a woman weeping with grief. He called out, and the dream shifted to show the back of a woman with soft ginger hair looking out to the ocean before her as she whispered a name again and again in agonising loss.

"Odysseus... Odysseus.... Odysseus."

Then she was gone too, and Nicos was stood on the prow of a ship, looking at an island appearing out of the mist. It sang to him, calling him to it.

The sound of a foot stepping on a branch snapped Nicos out of his dreams. He was on his feet in seconds, pulling his sword from its sheath that lay on the floor by him. The wolf, too, was up, alert, and scanning the trees around them. Theron moved closer to Nicos as the other wolves came out from the cave, surrounding them both in a protective circle. Every direction was covered by a set of eyes. Nicos listened carefully. Nothing. Whatever or whoever snapped that twig had clocked their mistake. It had to be a human. He couldn't deny the nerves that were fluttering in his stomach. For the first time, he felt that he was being hunted.

It's bandits. No one knows I am here. It has to be bandits.

The wolves, Theron and Nicos, held their position longer, making sure they were in the clear. Nicos moved first. He kicked some dirt over what remained of the fire and started to gear up Theron.

"Will you scout ahead for me?" Nicos addressed the large dark grey alpha wolf. It grunted and moved with its pack into the trees. "Be safe. Okay Theron, I think we should ride as quickly as we can."

Theron gave a whinny.

A brown wolf broke the trees by the pond and beckoned with its head. Nicos thanked it and pulled himself up onto the saddle, nudging Theron to follow the wolf. They were barely a few strides away from the cave when Nicos stopped Theron and slipped down. He moved towards a thorny shrub, watching a piece of grey fabric flapping in the wind. Nicos looked around, noticing a set of footprints and tracks of a horse. It headed back in the way of the road. Someone had been so close to him. His eyes scanned through the forest, trying to spot anything. It seemed empty, except for the deer he saw grazing peacefully.

Just get going.

As he got back up on Theron, he noticed that all the wolves had gathered around him again. This made him smile. How could he be nervous with a pack of wolves as an escort? Theron picked up his pace as they headed further up into the forest, away from the road and whomever may be there.

12

Nicos had been riding for four days, and he felt the aches and pains in his body. He hadn't slept in a bed since the night at Jocasta's place, and he could really feel the effect of sleeping on the hard earth each night. The wolves had stayed with him for quite a while after he left the cover of the forest. A group of bandits that had been lying in wait for a victim to rob ran screaming after they jumped out and saw a young man on a black horse flanked on either side by wolves. Nicos had laughed at how high the men screamed. It then occurred to him that when passing travellers and through villages, his canine entourage would raise questions. He bid them goodbye and watched as they scurried off into the hills.

As the day carried on, Nicos came up on an elderly woman struggling to carry a heavy basket of freshly harvested wheat. She was bent double under the weight of it.

"Please allow me to help you," Nicos said as he jumped from the horse's back. The stranger looked at him with grateful eyes.

"I couldn't ask that of you, young one." Her voice was raspy with age.

"You did not ask, I offered." Nicos smiled as he helped take the basket from her back. Theron lowered himself on Nicos command, and he helped the old woman into the saddle.

"What a fine beast," she complimented, "I have never seen a horse look so well." Theron shook his mane with pride.

"May I know your name?" Nicos asked as they began walking on.

"I am Merope and who is my hero?" Merope smiled. Nicos liked her smile, it was warm and made her eyes wrinkle.

"Nicos."

The three wandered a mile along the road. Merope told Nicos of how her husband, Dimitrios, had met when they were young, and both had been struck by the arrows of Eros. Usually, Dimitrios would be carrying the harvest back, but it had ripened earlier than expected, and he had been burnt, putting out a fire that had broken out in their stable. She told how he had bravely rescued their horses but at the expense of his hands. Merope directed them to take a dirt track that would lead them to her home. Sure enough, at the end of the track was a small farmhouse with a burnt stable just off to the left. A man of Merope's age was perched on a stool just outside the door, his hands wrapped in cloth. Dimitrios.

"Have you finally traded me in for a younger man?" Dimitrios greeted.

"Not just yet." Merope chuckled.

Nicos dropped the basket of harvest by Dimitrios, who thanked him profusely, then aided Merope to dismount Theron. Merope ordered Nicos to put Theron in the stable so he might eat and drink, before telling him, in no uncertain terms, that he must join them for dinner. A cooked meal? How could he say no? Theron settled easily enough amongst the two older horses and mules that were already in the stable. Nicos saw other baskets of harvest behind the house, so without hesitation, he picked up the basket he had left out front and placed it with the others. Both Dimitrios and Merope thanked him again and bid him come inside.

"I am afraid it isn't much." Merope said as she handed Nicos a steaming bowl of porridge.

"It is more than enough." Nicos took the bowl gratefully.

"Nonsense," Dimitrios said, "I am indebted to you…"

"Nicos, dear," his wife informed him.

"Nicos. I would usually help my beloved Merope, but my hands are of little use." He raised his bandaged hands, the wrappings looked old and muddied with dried blood. Merope sat beside him and fed him his porridge first before tucking into her own. It warmed Nicos' heart to see such honest, kind love. He ate his porridge hungrily, relishing the warmth that spilled down his throat. Once they had all finished, Nicos ran from the room. He ran out to get his satchel that he had left outside with Theron's saddle and his bow and arrows. He rummaged in it and pulled out a small jar. Nicos bounded back into the house to find a slightly wide-eyed Dimitrios.

"May I?" Nicos asked as he sat opposite the old man.

Dimitrios nodded. The young man took the old man's hands in his and gently began to unbandage them. The smell of burnt flesh filled his nostrils.

"They are not pretty to look at," Dimitrios said, looking down in embarrassment.

Nicos looked at the raw, red hands of his generous host and turned them over, inspecting the burns. Merope looked over his shoulder. He opened the jar to see a soft, rose-coloured paste. Quickly, he scooped some into his palms and rubbed his hands together, spreading the paste. He offered a gentle smile to a curious-looking Dimitrios as he placed his hands onto the burnt ones.

Dimitrios had expected searing pain at Nicos' touch, but instead a cooling sensation spread from the contact. A sigh of relief left his mouth as Merope watched the pain leave her husband's face. After a few minutes, Nicos let go of the other man's hands to reveal the skin looking more normal. Dimitrios flexed his fingers and let out a sound of excitement as they moved without pain.

"How…?" Merope marvelled.

"It's a simple salve," Nicos replied modestly.

"This is not simple at all, surely it has been touched by Asclepius himself," Dimitrios said.

"Not at all, I made it myself. I can tell you how if you like. Just in case." Nicos was enjoying their reaction. The hunters of Artemis had quickly become used to his potions. "I really had better be on my way."

"Please stay with us tonight, it is the least we can do." Merope insisted as Dimitrios eagerly poured them some wine, delighted that he was able to use his hands once more.

"I don't want to put you out, really, I am quite happy sleeping under the stars." Nicos put up a faux show of resistance.

"That is enough answering back, my lad," Dimitrios scolded playfully. "We have a bed spare, and you will take it for tonight."

"Well, I suppose that's settled then."

The three of them sat talking around the table until the moon was high in the sky. At some point, Dimitrios had slipped out to feed the horses and returned with Nicos' satchel, bow, and arrows. He followed the old man up some rickety wooden stairs to be shown into a small room with a bed. Nicos beamed at the sight of it, and with a kiss on the cheek from Merope, they all said good night to each other. As soon as the door was closed behind him, he flopped on the bed and was asleep in seconds.

The dream that had been haunting him since he left Athens came again in the same broken pieces. An island, bones of children, Cerberus, the ginger-haired woman, and the dragons. It made no sense to him. It never got any clearer. He knew that it must mean something. But what?

It was early when Nicos woke up. He stretched, feeling much of his aches and pains vanish. For a brief moment, he forgot he was inside a house, and only when he swung his legs off the bed to sit up was he fully aware of his surroundings. Downstairs, he could hear Merope and Dimitrios talking, but quickly he was aware theirs wasn't the only voices he could hear. In an instant, he was at the door, silently pulling it open so that he could listen.

"You don't want another fire started, do you, old man?" A rough, brutish-sounding man threatened.

"We gave you all we had last time; come back after the harvest season when we…" Dimitrios was cut off and let out a yelp.

"You are lying to us, old man. Where did that handsome black horse come from if you gave us all you had? Perhaps you need some motivation."

Merope screamed.

Nicos thought for a moment. He worked through the layout of the house and how best to engage the intruders with as little risk as possible to his hosts. Slinging his bow and arrows over his shoulder, Nicos made his way out of the window and climbed down the side of the house, dropping soundlessly to the floor. The front door was open, and through it, Nicos finally got sight of the invading men. The man in charge was bald and had two fingers missing from his left hand and an axe fixed to his back.

One man, with his back to the door, had Merope against the wall, his hand around her throat. The other two, who couldn't have been much older than himself, held Dimitrios up by either arm as their leader loomed over him. Dimitrios had a cut on his cheek, and already a black eye was forming. Nicos steadied his rage and, with expert skill, notched an arrow, pulled the string back, and released it.

The man holding Merope screamed. He let go of her as the arrow lodged into his shoulder. The others quickly drew their weapons and turned to face the door. Dimitrios, free from their hold, crawled over to his wife and held her to him.

"Who do you have here, old man?" The bald man asked angrily. "Only a coward hides his face!" He then shouted towards the door.

"Only a coward threatens an elderly couple. Come out and face me if you dare." Nicos shouted back, readying another arrow.

The bald brute grabbed Dimitrios by the hair and pushed him before him as a shield. His band of cohorts stepped out of the front door, flanking him on either side. The sun broke from behind a cloud, and its light fell on Nicos, making him look like he was glowing. The four thugs stared at the stranger with the bow, armed and ready.

"Are these horses yours?" Nicos asked politely.

"Who, in the name of the gods, are you?" The bald man asked.

Run, Nicos thought, and without hesitation, the horses turned galloping off down the dirt track. The man he had shot called after them in vain.

"Release my friend; leave here quietly, and no one else gets hurt." Nicos said sweetly.

"Do you know who I am?" The lead ruffian said.

"Does it matter?" Nicos shrugged.

"This is Basileus," the wounded man declared, as though the name alone should inspire some kind of fear.

"Lovely to meet you. Now about my friend…"

"I will cut his throat before you can release that arrow," Basileus snarled.

"Do you want to bet?" Nicos answered coolly.

Basileus laughed coldly. Then, deciding his life was worth more than Dimitrios, he pushed the old man forward. Nicos dropped his bow to catch the stumbling man. The thugs saw their chance. They rushed at Nicos, swords drawn. Instinctively, Nicos moved Dimitrios out of the way, just in time for a sword to clunk into the ground. The men slashed and stabbed at the unarmed Nicos, who dodged and weaved like water flowing around rocks. Basileus watched in awe and alarm, his mind trying to make sense of the man before him.

One of the younger-looking men thrust his sword right at Nicos' heart, it would have killed him if he hadn't caught the blade between his palms. The shock on the grunts face was palpable. Nicos kicked into the guy's stomach, winding him, causing him to drop his weapon. It was in Nicos' hand before it hit the ground. It only took him a few seconds to disarm the remaining two. As they cowered back, Nicos turned to face Basileus, who held his hands up in defeat.

"I think it's time you left, and I never want to see you here again." Nicos said firmly.

"As you wish." Basileus said. He beckoned his grunts to follow him, one went to pick up his sword, but Nicos tutted and shook his head. They were just past him when Nicos' hair stood on end.

"LOOK OUT!" Dimitrios shouted.

Basileus had drawn a dagger from his side and was bringing it down, aiming for Nicos' back. He wasn't fast enough. Nicos dropped and spun, kicking his leg out, tripping Basileus. As he fell, he lost grip of his dagger, sending it flying in the air above him. He landed with a thump, only to see the dagger that was meant for Nicos falling towards him. Nicos caught it inches from his throat.

"I asked that you leave." Nicos' eyes were wild, sending terror rippling through Basileus's body.

"I will go, I will go," he pleaded.

Nicos stood, his wild eyes staring at the bandits as they helped up their boss.

"I will see you run from this place." Nicos' voice was cold and dangerous. Above them, birds began to circle, first one and then more and more still, all different types. Nicos pointed at the men before him and whispered one word to them.

"Run."

At the very same moment, the birds descended in a fury upon the bandits, their beaks pecking and claws scratching at them as they ran. Only as they reached the road proper did the birds abandon their pursuit, though the men didn't stop running for a long time after. Nicos came back to himself when he felt the soft, warm hand of Merope on his elbow. He watched as the birds dispersed in different directions, as though nothing had happened.

"You are a blessed child of the gods!" Merope bowed and kissed his hands.

"No, please don't. I am just Nicos." His voice was shaky.

"Come, let us have some breakfast." Dimitrios said in a fatherly fashion, putting an arm around Nicos.

"I should be on my way." Nicos protested weakly but let himself be taken inside. Merope made quick work of righting the chairs and fixing a plate of fruits and bread on the table. Nicos sat in a daze. What had just happened? Never in all his years had he commanded animals in such quantity. He had always been able to commune with and understand them, but that, with the birds, was something entirely new.

They ate in silence. Merope and Dimitrios, unsure of what to say, watched Nicos with a look of concern. Not concern for themselves but for the boy that suddenly looked younger than when he arrived.

"I have never done that before." Nicos offered into the silence.

"Fight a group of nasty bandits?" Dimitrios answered lightly. Nicos couldn't help the corners of his mouth curl up in a small smile.

"With the birds."

"Oh that?" Merope said, "Was it unusual? Birds have always been protective creatures… we have a rooster that gets very aggressive when provoked."

Nicos laughed, and so did Dimitrios. There was nothing more to say then, he thought. He was overwhelmed once again by the simple beauty of their kindness and generosity. As they finished, Merope wrapped up the leftovers and insisted he take them with him on his journey.

"Where are you headed, my lad?" Dimitrios asked as he helped saddle up Theron.

"Pelion." Nicos didn't want to lie to them.

"You won't have long then, you see…" Dimitrios pointed to a mountain that was just visible on a clear day. "That there is Mount Pelion."

Nicos had no idea he was so close. A thought occurred to him.

"Could I leave Theron with you?" He asked.

Dimitrios nodded. Theron looked haughtily over his shoulder and gave a huff. It had occurred to him that riding in on a horse to meet a centaur might somehow seem improper. He gave the horse a last goodbye, sweetened with the gift of an apple to Theron. Nicos then slung his bow and quiver over his shoulder, and with his satchel in place, he gave his farewell to Merope and Dimitrios.

"Thank you again for your hospitality. Hestia will bless you; I am sure." Nicos said.

"We have been blessed enough with you crossing my wife's path yesterday," Dimitrios said as he gave Nicos a fatherly hug.

"I doubt those men will be back, but if they do…"

"Hush." Merope interrupted as she embraced him. "It won't take long for the story to spread about what happened here; you have ensured our safety for the rest of our lives."

It gave Nicos a sense of relief to know this. In such a short time, he had come to care so deeply for these people. Thea had always said his heart was too big.

"If we had been gifted with a son, I would hope that they would be like you." Merope said, taking his face in her hands, and, with a final kiss on his cheek, they watched him walk off down the track towards Mount Pelion.

13

It already seemed so long ago that Nicos had left the only home he had ever known, though in truth it had only been a little over a week. He found himself thinking of what Thea and Korinna would be up to and if they missed him as much as he missed them. Zander crossed his mind too. In fact, as Nicos passed through the last village near the base of Mount Pelion, he could have sworn that he saw him riding off in the direction he had just come from. He shook his head at the silliness of the thought. Zander would be back in Athens, and Nicos doubted he would be thinking about him at all.

Making his way through the village, he picked up parts of conversations, speaking news of a strange traveller on a black horse that commanded the birds. It had spread just as quickly as Merope had said. He overheard others gossiping and speculating who it might be.

"It could be one of the gods in disguise," a drunk man spluttered.

"Right enough, probably looking to torment us in some new way." His equally drunk friend agreed as he relieved himself against a wall.

The gossip flittered around, making Nicos feel both relieved and anxious. The relief was for Merope and

Dimitrios. They would be safe, especially as with each new retelling, the bird man seemed to get taller, the birds got bigger, and the bandits grew in number. The anxiety came from doing exactly what he was told not to do by Thea, Hermia, and Artemis which was to draw attention to himself. He managed to make some peace with it as he knew that there was no other way to help those who had been so generous to him. Also, he thought, the thing with the birds really wasn't planned. He still didn't quite understand how that had happened.

Chiron will help me find these answers. He has to!

Once out of the village and away from prying eyes, Nicos let himself fall into the grass, letting out a great sigh of relief. He had almost made it. He still had to make his way up the mountain and then find Chiron, but right now he basked in his small victory of reaching his destination. The sun was high, and the cool shade of the trees that sprawled up the mountain offered a blessed respite; so too did the last dregs of his water from his waterskin. He looked up into the trees, trying to see if there might be a clue as to Chiron's whereabouts, but nothing. Even when he shared eyes with a hovering buzzard above, he couldn't see anything.

On we go, then.

Before standing, he pulled off his sandals and tucked them into his satchel. It had been far too long since he walked barefoot in a forest. With a fresh sense of purpose, Nicos began to make his way through the trees and up Mount Pelion. Each time his bare soles connected with the mountain forest floor, it sent a burst of energy through him, as though it was trying to heal any ache or pain that lingered in his body. For a short time on his ascent, Nicos forgot why he was there, lost in the enjoyment of being in a place that reminded him so much of home. He was so lost in memories of times foraging with Korinna or racing Thea through the trees that he didn't hear that someone had fallen in step a little way behind him.

"I had expected the Son of Circe to arrive on horseback, not wandering like a dryad," a smooth, deep voice said.

Nicos turned quickly and was quite speechless at the sight before him. He had never seen a centaur before, mostly because there weren't many left. Nicos looked up into a violet-eyed bearded human face that held the secret signs of age, soft wrinkles by the eyes and grey hair speckled through the black beard and long plaited hair. He marvelled at the bare, scarred olive-skinned torso that blended into the sleek body of a dapple-grey horse, a long, black tail with wisps of grey swishing behind him.

"Master Chiron." Nicos bowed.

"I am no one's master, nor is anyone mine," Chiron replied, his voice like silk. "Have you travelled all this way on foot?"

Nicos shook his head, "No, only the last day. I left my horse with friends."

"Why?" asked Chiron.

"Honestly, I thought it might be rude somehow, to come in riding a horse, when you are…" he was cut off by the deep, joyful belly laugh that burst from Chiron. Nicos flushed with embarrassment.

"Never has any mortal been so courteous before. You really are unique, aren't you?" Chiron chuckled. "I have no problem with mortal men riding horses, as long as those they ride are treated fairly. Come, let us get you settled, we have much to discuss."

Chiron and Nicos walked side by side for an hour or so, higher up the mountainside. Now and then the centaur would point out some herbs, impressed when Nicos could name them as well as the properties they held. He enjoyed it more when they came across something Nicos didn't know, not because he enjoyed knowing more, but because he liked to see the joy and fascination on the young man's face. Chiron promised to teach Nicos all he knew of plants and herbs if, in turn, Nicos would share some of his potions and salves with him.

Chiron's home was set into a hidden pasture that, he informed Nicos, could not be seen or found by anyone mortal or divine unless he wished it. A bargain he had made with the Olympians at the fall of the Titans. In return, he would train their heroes from time to time. The pasture was idyllic.

The mountain stream trickled through the middle of the grassy area that was littered with wild forest flowers. Against the rock was a fire pit and a patch of grass to its right, which seemed permanently flattened; this was where Chiron slept. Just behind that, the mountain side caved in on itself a little, forming a shallow cave, so shallow that when the fire was lit, it danced along the back wall. Even now, in the soft light of dusk, you could see all the way inside.

"Inside there," Chiron pointed into the shallow opening in the mountain, "is where you will sleep. Leave your weapons in there, and only get them when I instruct. That is my only rule, and never lie to me, and I shall never lie to you."

Nicos nodded politely and went to set his belongings down. The furs that lined the floor were soft beneath his feet. He knew he would be most comfortable here. Chiron had got a fire going and was in the beginning of cooking some sort of stew.

"Why don't you wash yourself before we eat?" Chiron instructed.

Nicos didn't need to be told twice; he had wanted to wash himself since Chiron found him. In no time at all, Nicos had stripped off his clothes and was in the fresh, cold mountain stream, dunking his entire head under the water and staying there for as long as he could. When he broke the surface, he felt like he was breathing for the first time in a long while. There was no stress or threat looming. Well, there was, he knew that really, but here in this stream on Mount Pelion, he felt free.

At some point in his bathing, Chiron had taken his sweaty, dirt-covered maroon chiton and replaced it with a new one of brown and green. It held a similarity to that of his former hunter's tunic. The smell of whatever Chiron was cooking filled his nostrils, and reluctantly, he pulled himself from the water. He sat by the fire, letting himself dry. Chiron draped the fur of a bear over his naked body.

"It gets cold up here." He said.

The centaur moved to serve up a bowl of steaming broth in a handmade wooden bowl and spoon. Nicos ate it down hungrily and didn't refuse second or third helpings. Above them, the sky danced with constellations as the sound of the creatures of the night could be heard grunting, hooting, and snuffling in the forest around them. Being here felt so much like being back home in the hunters' village. A pang of sadness stung his chest.

Placing his bowl on the floor beside him, he pulled on the fresh tunic Chiron had given him, making sure to thank him for the gift.

"Now that you are dressed and fed, it is time to talk about more serious things," Chiron said. "I am not one to meddle in the business of gods, but Apollo has been a friend of mine for longer than I care to share." A cheeky grin crossed his handsome face, his bright eyes glittering in the firelight.

"If I had my way, Chiron, I would not meddle either." Nicos said with the deepest sincerity.

"Alas, sweet one, you may not have that luxury. Though you are outside of fate, it seems many others have theirs tied to you. Even the stars show me so many different futures."

Nicos looked up, as Chiron did, at the vast, starlit sky.

"I will teach you what I know of stargazing over time, though no mortal has ever been able to master it like we centaurs," Chiron said with a quiet pride. "Though you may be more adept than others, with Apollo's blood in your veins. What gifts have you inherited from your divine parentage?"

Nicos shrugged. "I'm not sure. Artemis says my gift with the bow comes from her, I never miss my mark. I have a sight like hers too. I don't know if I have anything of Apollo in me, that is to say, nothing I can see."

Chiron's violet eyes stared straight into Nicos, as though he was looking into his very soul.

"I can see the light of Apollo in you even now. It will show itself in time. Your knowledge of plants and potions comes, of course, from your mother."

"Circe? Did you know her?" Nicos asked, desperate to know more about the woman.

"I met her once, many lifetimes ago, in the age of the Titans. It was custom that when a new Titan child was born, they came to the centaurs to have their stars plotted and futures glimpsed. However, after the great war and castration of Kronos, that tradition disappeared. That is, until those Titans that allied with Zeus were allowed to have children again. Helios bought many of his litter to me, including your mother. In her stars, I saw her skill with witchcraft, though it meant nothing to Helios, as witchery hadn't really been seen in the world, and the glimpses that had, were for lesser deities.

"Perhaps that was best, as I believe if he had known of how powerful she would be, he would have used her for his own gains. The thing all gods crave most is power, Olympian or Titan. I had wanted desperately to offer my guardianship of the child; I knew of all the suffering she would endure, but only through that suffering would she become the great witch she was destined to be." Chiron watched a pained expression pass over the young man's face. "You think I should have offered?"

Nicos gave a slight shrug.

"You, my dear boy, are the only being outside of fate. What was written for Circe had to be. It is cruel; I won't deny it, but without it, we rarely see what we can become. I am sad to say that I am sure you will have a tough road ahead. Still, that is not for worrying on now. I am tired, and you must be too; let us to bed," Chiron yawned.

Nicos was tired. It took him no time at all to get comfortable on the furs, arranging one as a pillow. The steady breathing of Chiron lulled him into a deep sleep. The dream came again, still in its broken form, though something was different. When the image of the misty island came into view, he could hear a voice. A woman's voice. It was calling to him.

"Come home… Come home, my son…" the mysterious voice echoed in his head. It lingered even as he woke. His eyes scanned the trees in vain, hoping he might see the owner of the voice. Nothing. Nicos got himself up and stretched, feeling his bare feet in the dewy grass. He moved to the stream to splash cold water on his face, trying to get the voice out of his mind. Only when Chiron tapped him on the shoulder, making him jump, did he feel like his mind was his own again.

"I didn't mean to frighten you, only I was calling your name, and… are you alright?" Chiron's voice was warm, like being wrapped in a thick fleece.

"Yes… sorry. Bad dreams," Nicos answered.

"Dreams should never be ignored, Son of Circe. Will you tell me?" Chiron asked.

Nicos nodded.

Over a breakfast of wild berries and fresh goats milk, Nicos told the centaur everything. The dragons, the island, the woman calling for Odysseus, Cerberus, the bones of children, adding on finally about the island, and the voice that had only begun appearing last night. Chiron thought silently with a wrinkled brow for a long while.

"Will you give me a little time? Some pieces I understand, others less so." Chiron asked thoughtfully.

"Of course," Nicos replied, relieved that the wise centaur understood some of what he had shared.

"Thank you."

Nicos had expected that Chiron would speak to him about his dream later that day, however, it wasn't to be. It was several months, in fact, before he even brought it up again. In the meantime, Chiron had fixed a poultice to keep the dream at bay so that Nicos might rest better. Their days were filled with various lessons from the wise centaur. Nicos learnt to name the new mountain flora and fauna, though it shocked Chiron that instinctively Nicos knew what properties they had, even suggesting new potions and remedies they could aid with.

Chiron, in turn, was learning from Nicos, something he hadn't experienced in several ages. The pair shared their knowledge freely and excitedly. Chiron was fascinated when Nicos would share eyes with the mountain beasts, watching the brilliant eyes of the young man change to those of a hawk, lion, goat, and serpent. Over the months, Nicos had begun to learn how to control the creature to which he was linked, making them go in different directions. He had even sent fifteen or so snakes through a bandit camp a little way down the mountainside. Chiron found it most entertaining.

They had begun to discover what Nicos had inherited from Apollo's blood. It was evident he was gifted musically, as with every instrument Chiron carved and passed to him, he could play some pretty enchanting little tune. Chiron had also deduced that Nicos had some gift of prophecy, saying his dreams were surely pointing him towards something. When Nicos pressed him further to see if he had any idea what they meant, Chiron dismissed him. The final gift of Apollo was still waiting to reveal itself, though on a cold and dark winter morning, they got a glimpse. Nicos was struggling to get the fire started.

"The kindling is too damp, and this wind!" Nicos grunted in frustration. Chiron had made him a winter outfit made of mountain lion fur that barely kept out the biting cold.

"You will get it, my lad," Chiron encouraged as he draped another fur over the shivering Nicos. "Focus."

"I am focusing!" He bit back a little harder than he meant.

"Close your eyes; breathe," Chiron instructed. "see the fire ablaze in your mind and strike the stones."

Nicos closed his eyes and took a deep breath. He could see the fire in his mind. The visual was so strong, his hands even felt warm. Smiling, he opened his eyes. Chiron was staring at him, a slightly stunned expression on his face. Nicos followed his eyeline down to his hands. The palms of them were glowing as white light danced around his fingers. Focusing, Nicos turned them towards the kindling. It started to steam, then smoke, and then it caught. The flames stirred, and the heat was immediate. It was hotter than normal fire and didn't blow around in the wind as flames usually do. Chiron let out a cheer, and Nicos beamed.

"Apollo's gift of light," Chiron declared.

Nicos got a quick grasp, as he did with most things, of how he could call up the divine light and put it to use. It proved to be a little more of a destructive learning process. Several times he started small forest fires and burnt himself often. Chiron didn't mind this so much as he got to practice making the burn salve that Nicos taught him. One evening, Chiron told of how Apollo could create arrows out of light, as well as other weapons. This inspired Nicos greatly. With the permission of the centaur, he picked up his bow the next day and tried to do the same. He tried again and again and again. Nothing happened.

"It will take time," Chiron reassured, "or, perhaps, it is not meant to be."

The icy cold of winter on the mountain gave way to the fresh breath of spring. Mount Pelion felt alive with the first flowers and the mewling of young wolves, deer, and goats that surrounded the home of Chiron. Nicos' understanding of his gifts and witchcraft had grown, though he still couldn't manage to craft an arrow out of light, and still Chiron hadn't answered his dreams. Being on the mountain felt like home, and Nicos had almost forgotten why he had come. Almost.

The first morning of the seventh month began like any other. Helios was creeping over the trees as Eos, Goddess of Dawn, painted the sky in shades of pastel pink. Nicos had woken with a start and was on his feet, bow in hand, in the flash of a second.

"Chiron?" he whispered, seeing the centaur too, was on his feet, bow ready. "What is it, Chiron?" Nicos asked as he stood facing out into the trees.

"Who do you see out there?" Chiron's voice was low.

Nicos focused his sight forward and searched the woodland as far as he could.

There!

About fifty metres or so from them was a man. A bare-chested figure was cutting through the trees. He was beautiful. There was something else, something that Nicos was struggling to place. It was the way the figure moved. He had only seen one other person move in such a way.

"It's a god!" Nicos exclaimed quietly. His fingers gripped tighter on his bow.

"Can you see who?" Chiron asked, his voice dangerously calm.

Nicos shook his head.

"Stay here." Chiron ordered as he galloped towards the invading Olympian. Nicos kept his eyes fixed on Chiron. He watched as the centaur ran with incredible speed and grace, ducking and weaving around the trees. He watched as he came upon the stranger,. They talked, and both wore expressions of concern. Then they were heading back towards Nicos. Slowly, he lowered his bow as the centaur and the stranger broke the treeline.

"Nicos, let me introduce you to Apollo," Chiron gestured to the beautiful man on his right.

"The honour is all mine, Son of Circe." Apollo gave a small bow of the head.

14

The forge of Hephaestus was buried in the depths of Mount Olympus, its fires always burning. The heat of the place was as hot as the sun. If any mortal were to step inside without an invitation, they would feel their skin melt from their bones. Hephaestus, however, would tell you the forge was like a warm summer day, in fact, it was said that outside of the forge, he always felt a chill prick his skin. The forge was filled with glistening weapons of immense beauty hanging from the walls. Others lay discarded in a pile, waiting to be melted down and remade. Very few of his fellow Olympians ever came to his forge, and he liked it that way. Here, he was the master. He sat now in an unassuming stone chair, drinking a cup of nectar, his mind lost in thought. So lost, he didn't even notice Aphrodite enter.

Aphrodite glided into the forge, a delicate smile lighting up her face. It is true that at first there had been no love between her and Hephaestus. Their marriage had been one of convenience and was completely undesired by Aphrodite. Zeus was bored of the squabbling gods, so he had ordered Hephaestus to take her as his bride, to the absolute delight of the God of Blacksmiths and Fire.

"I will not marry that hunchback! Give me another Zeus! Ares, give me him," Aphrodite protested.

"Yes, give her to me, father," Ares cheered.

"My word is final! You will marry Hephaestus and be happy about it." Zeus ordered.

Hephaestus bowed to her, and she completely disregarded him for centuries. It wasn't until Hephaestus trapped her and Ares in an unbreakable chain net as they lay together that she even noticed him properly. The fire, passion, and love he held for her. It was entrancing to the Goddess of Love. It was entrancing because she had nothing to do with it. His love came from his own heart, his own choice, completely free of her control. From that moment, she was devoted to her husband–well, as devoted as gods can be. Sure, she still slept with mortals, but that didn't mean anything to the pair.

Aphrodite fell in love with the imperfect nature of the godly blacksmith. Once she saw ugliness, but now she saw bravery and honesty. Even now, as she stood watching her thought-filled husband, her heart gave the same leap it had done for thousands of years.

"I hate to interrupt your ruminations, sweet husband," Aphrodite said in her soft, lilting voice.

Hephaestus's eyes flicked up to see her. He stood and bowed to her as he always had, facing her with a smile that was only for her. "It is no matter at all when one as beautiful as you is my interruption." He kissed her sweetly. "What brings you into my forge? Do you need something crafting my love?"

"No. I wondered if I might share some worries that have been dancing around my mind with you."

Hephaestus took her by the hand, leading her to a polished marble throne with a plush pink cushion and her emblem carved into its back. Aphrodite looked at her husband with admiration as she sat. The throne had been made by Hephaestus when they first got married, and this was the first time she had ever seen it. He took his place again in his chair of stone.

"What is it my love?" Hephaestus asked.

"It's Zeus. I think he goes too far with his demands. He is driving a wedge between us all." She spoke quickly, as though Zeus could appear at any moment.

Hephaestus furrowed his brow.

"I know that he is afraid of the witch's child, but his fear is destroying us. What he did to Apollo with the Oracle was not right. We have never involved ourselves in each other's business like this," Aphrodite continued. "Then I have heard rumours that he may ban us from going down amongst the mortals completely."

"From whom?" Hephaestus looked concerned.

"Demeter. She overheard Athena talking with Zeus, Hera, and Ares."

Hephaestus thought for a moment and answered, "He cannot dictate to us what we do nor where we go. It breaks the code of Olympia that was written at the beginning of our reign. That is what separated us from the Titans."

Aphrodite nodded her head in agreement.

"He worries so much about the war coming that he does not see how he is causing its beginning." Hephaestus said in a solemn voice.

***

"But what does Hades think of the matter?" Demeter asked her daughter, Persephone, as they walked through a field of wheat, ripening the crop as they passed. Her daughter looked a lot like her, with vibrant red hair and bright green eyes, though her skin was pale and white as alabaster. She was dressed in a burnt orange dress that trailed behind her, whilst her mother, Demeter, wore one of simple beige.

"He doesn't think much of it, mother." Her reply was very matter of fact.

Demeter gave her a pained look.

"Hades does not count himself an Olympian," Persephone continued, "so cares not of some war. He has always said that Zeus' arrogance, pride, and fear will be the fall of Olympus. I agree with him on that."

They crossed into another pasture, Demeter mulling over the truths Persephone had shared. Zeus had always been a hothead, but then which god wasn't? Only most of the hotheadedness had been directed towards the mortals. Now it seemed that it had shifted towards those with divine blood. She thought of the night Zeus had gone to Circe's Island.

He was driven by pride, and dare she say it, his fears. There had never been anything before that could rival an Olympian. That was a frightening thought, but Circe had never done anything to them. They had all nearly forgotten her after she was banished. Also, she was only a witch, and really, they had never been a threat. Even less so when Hecate, the Goddess of witchcraft, had disappeared.

"I think," Persephone said, "the war has already begun. Apollo disobeys the king; Artemis defies him, and here you are questioning him." There was no judgement in

Persephone's voice, but Demeter felt as though she had been scolded.

"Yes, I am questioning him. I fear he may divide us in his actions. Some of us believe we should find the child of Circe and win him to our side. Others believe we should obliterate them as we did their mother," said Demeter; she had come to a standstill and taken her daughter's hands in hers. "I must leave my sweet child; we are being summoned. I shall see you before you return to Hades." She kissed Persephone's cheek and turned into the air.

Everyone was in place as Demeter, the last to arrive, sat down. The air was thick with tension, no one spoke. Athena was once again in whispered council with Zeus.

"Will you keep us waiting long, brother?" Poseidon's annoyance echoed around the pantheon.

Zeus waved his hand in dismissal at his brother. The sea water at Poseidon's feet crashed with angry waves. Somewhere below, off the shore of Mykonos, the sea raged.

"Let us drink then, whilst we wait on our king," Dionysus said as goblets of sweet red wine appeared in the other god's hands. Poseidon drank his down, throwing the goblet in the direction of Zeus. It clattered and clunked noisily to his feet. Dionysus beckoned with his hand, and the remaining goblets disappeared from the others. Zeus gave a thunderous look at Poseidon as he rose to his feet.

"You forget yourself, brother. You may be king of the sea, but here and always I am king of all of you," Zeus' threatened in a deep, rumbling voice.

Poseidon bit back a retort as he continued to stare directly back at his brother. Hera gave a polite clearing of her throat.

Zeus turned away from Poseidon and began addressing the gathered assembly.

"I thank you all for setting your spies to work in finding the bastard child of the witch," Zeus began, forcing a lightness into his voice. "I have called you all here so that I may set in the new rules of Olympus."

A disgruntled murmur rippled around him.

"These rules are to keep us all safe. You are no longer to mix with the mortals of Greece. No more divine offspring unless I have decreed it. Any children you have had, I want their names and lineage."

Eruptions of outrage came first from Poseidon, followed quickly by Apollo, Artemis, and Aphrodite. Demeter sat in silence. The divide had begun.

"How dare you decree who we bed?" Poseidon roared.

"I will not be bound to this place when I belong in the wild!" protested Artemis.

"The mortals need us! We cannot abandon them because you are afraid of some child." Apollo shouted. That did it. Zeus turned on them all in a terrible rage, the sky above them turned the darkest grey and thundered.

"YOU ARE LUCKY. I DON'T BIND YOU ALL HERE AND NOW!!!" Zeus bellowed. "I FEAR NOTHING."

Poseidon roared with laughter, "Liar. You may be king, brother, but your actions are those of a coward. This child is no threat to Olympus. We are gods!" With a sudden rush of water, Poseidon was gone. Ares stood with a fierce, blood thirsty look on his face.

"I stand with you, father; I can manage my wars from here and gladly give you my descendants amongst men," said Ares. The thunder eased slightly. Hera stood to echo Ares's sentiment, as did Dionysus. Zeus turned to face Aphrodite and Hephaestus. They looked at one another and stood.

"Father, we gladly give you our lineage but will not be banned from walking amongst the mortals." Hephaestus said plainly.

"You will do as I command!" Zeus rumbled.

The couple looked at one another again.

"For now... we will comply," Aphrodite replied.

Demeter looked up to see Zeus staring at her. All she could bring herself to do was give a curt nod. Athena, from her throne, agreed to the terms, though bargained that if a member of her parliament were to summon her, she would be allowed to go, to which Zeus agreed. He said that if any of their spies got wind of Circe's child, that they had his permission to go and then report straight back to him.

"I, of course, agree, father," Hermes said quite happily, "though it does make my job as leader of souls to Hades rather tricky."

"Obviously, you are allowed to come and go as needed, my boy," said Zeus.

Finally, his eyes turned to find the twins, Apollo, and Artemis, only to see their thrones empty.

15

The last few months had been wrought with fighting and division amongst the Olympians. He had known his decree against mixing with mortals would cause upset, but never had he expected outright descent. Poseidon had refused to return to Olympus until his brother regained his senses. This infuriated Zeus. He was within his senses, trying to protect them all. Until Circe's child was brought to him and dealt with, he had to control any more offspring. With the bloodlines, he thought, he could trace the type of mortals that came from whom. He had learnt quickly that Helios would no longer be allowed to have any more children, as any witch that had come to be in Greece had come from his bloodline.

He thought, too, about how close they had come to finding Circe's bastard child. The stories of a woman walking with a pack of wolves blurred with stories of a man commanding an army of birds had spread like wildfire throughout Greece. Athena's trusted Parliament was close on the trail of someone, a young man, but then it went cold. Although she had said there was a plan afoot to find them again, he just had to be patient. Patience was not a virtue that Zeus possessed. Still, here in the pool on Mount Dikte, he could wait.

Mount Dikte had always been a place of safety and contemplation for the King of Olympus. He had been smuggled here by his mother, Gaia, to save him from being eaten by his father, Kronos. Here he had been truly happy before fate came to claim him. Through every great struggle he had known, this is where he came for peace; rarely did any other Olympian come and bother him here. As he lounged in the cool water, two young nymphs combed his thick hair and fed him ambrosia. Another sat on a rock, playing a lyre, singing some soft song that charmed the birds into harmony.

A squeal and a splash brought Zeus out of his peace. The nymph on the rock was gone, and disappearing into the water were the two others that had been taking care of his hair.

"Do you always have to scare them off?" Zeus asked.

"Yes. I find it ever so funny," Hera answered.

She looked resplendent in her flowing purple and green gown, which shimmered like a peacock feather in the light. Zeus smiled, beckoning her to join him. Hera moved towards him to sit on the rock where the nymph had been moments before. She let her feet dip into the water. Zeus stared up at her, drinking in her beauty. He had always disagreed with Paris's choice. He had been asked to judge between Hera, Athena, and Aphrodite, which was the most beautiful. Paris had chosen Aphrodite, but to him, Hera was the most beautiful.

"Do you have news?" Zeus asked.

"Nothing new," Hera answered. "I do, however, come with an idea."

Zeus moved through the water to be by his wife's feet, taking one in his hand and massaging it gently.

Hera sighed at his touch.

"Tell me, my Queen," Zeus said.

"I have been thinking about something the moirai said. They spoke of the child being twice blessed, correct?"

Zeus nodded for her to continue.

"Well," she continued, "who is the father?"

Zeus looked at his wife with bright eyes. How could he have not thought of that? He pulled himself up out of the water and pulled Hera into a wet embrace, his naked body pressing into her. Hera couldn't help but laugh and push him off.

"You brilliant woman! If we find the father, we can…" Zeus stopped as a darker thought presented itself. "One of our own betrayed us."

Hera knew this when she arrived. "It would appear so."

Zeus roared in fearsome anger, causing a great storm to tear across the skies. As the thunder rolled, lightning flashed. Zeus and Hera vanished from the pool on Dikte and stepped into the Olympian palace. Hera fetched a white robe for her husband and dressed him. He threw lightning bolts out in different directions, each one aimed at an Olympian. Almost in unison, the pantheon was filled with stunned-looking gods, that was —all except Poseidon.

"What is the meaning of this father?" Ares shouted.

Zeus answered him with a deadly look, a look he shared with each god, as his eyes moved around them.

"We have a traitor amongst us," Zeus' voice was deep and threatening. "Which one of you lay with the witch?"

It took a moment for anyone to understand the accusation. When they did, the looks of incredulity rippled across the faces of Olympus. Ares roared with laughter at the thought. Aphrodite whispered to Hephaestus, who in turn whispered something back, their eyes occasionally darting around the faces of the others. Demeter sat silently, her eyes fixed on Apollo. Artemis saw this and moved to stand in her line of vision, locking eyes with the Goddess of the Harvest.

Demeter knows! Artemis' voice filled Apollo's head.

Zeus knows. He replied in kind.

"Well… I am waiting!" Zeus broke the silence.

"It sounds like you already know who it is, father?" laughed Ares, standing to survey the group.

Zeus, enraged, grabbed a lightning bolt and threw it at Ares, sending him crashing into a marble pillar behind him. The marble cracked as Ares lay crumpled at its base.

"I FAIL TO SEE WHATS FUNNY!" Zeus thundered, making the floor shake.

Hera and Athena had come to Zeus' side in an effort to temper him, whilst Aphrodite moved behind her husband and Demeter crept closer to Artemis. Dionysus put down his goblet of wine and sat up straight, whilst Hermes stopped hovering and took his seat. Fighting amongst the Olympians wasn't unheard of, over the years, they had all battled one another, but this was different. Ares still lay crumpled on the floor, knocked out cold, the smell of burning flesh filling the noses of all those present.

"Why don't you understand I am trying to protect us all? This child should never have come to be, and yet it is, and one of you is responsible. You have lied again and again. Speak up, coward!" Zeus' eyes were trained on Apollo.

"What if I did?" Apollo answered, stepping forward to face the wrath of the king.

"Why?" Hera asked, putting herself between Apollo and his father.

"Because I don't believe the child will be our downfall. At least not all of ours." Apollo answered pointedly. "Has it occurred to no one that this child may be our saviour?"

Artemis had seen what was coming before Apollo's last word left his mouth. Zeus' fingers had started to spark as he called a thunderbolt to his hand. He had stepped from behind Hera and launched it straight towards Apollo's heart. Artemis had just managed to push her brother out of the way as the lightning crackled past them, exploding his throne to pieces.

Apollo was gone, and in his place stood Artemis, her bow raised, aiming straight at her father.

"You would have killed him!" Artemis said with a dangerous voice.

"He would kill all of us!" Zeus answered, lightning still crackling between his fingers.

"So, will you kill me now?" She asked as her fingers pulled the bow string tighter.

"Lower your bow, daughter," Zeus answered through his teeth.

Artemis did not lower her weapon.

Who knows how long they would have stayed in this standoff if it hadn't been for Demeter coming to Artemis' side in an open declaration of defiance against Zeus.

"Demeter?" Hera asked as she stepped up beside her husband.

"This has gone too far," Demeter answered sternly.

Ares gave a groan as he started to come to; the sound made Zeus hesitate, and the lightning dissipated from his fingers.

"Sister, if you follow Apollo, then you betray Olympus like he has." Athena said coolly. She had been sitting on her throne this whole time, watching.

Artemis let out a small laugh and turned, lowering her bow. "If you only knew... *sister.*" With that, she was gone too.

Zeus slumped into his throne, his face fixed with a look of fury. He looked around at the smoking rubble of where he had missed Apollo, then at Demeter, then to Ares, who now stood up, his burnt flesh starting to heal.

"If anyone speaks to the traitor twins or aides them in any way, then you will be cast out of Olympus." Zeus' voice was cold.

Demeter looked around her and then, with a deep inhale, turned and was gone from the pantheon. Hephaestus took Aphrodite by the hand, and with a sad look, they too turned into the air and were gone.

It was silent then on Olympus for the longest time. Hera scowled from her place by Zeus' side, and Athena sat, her mind working out varying strategies and reasoning. She knew she was missing something and was determined to work it out. Dionysus and Hermes whispered quietly to each other, and Ares stood like a kicked dog, his fingers tracing the burn scar that now covered his neck and shoulder, it didn't seem to be fading.

"So," Zeus said quietly, "the war begins."

16

Mount Pelion no longer felt safe. Nicos had felt it since Apollo arrived, and so too, he guessed, had Chiron. The centaur had reassured him that Zeus wouldn't dare break his oath, as it was sworn on the Styx. Apollo and Chiron spent much of the day speaking about the confrontation and all that had been shared. He asked too about where the other Olympians stood.

"Artemis obviously stands with us, but I was gone before I could see —maybe none," Apollo said. He sounded weary. Chiron's brow wrinkled in thought, and then, in a way Nicos had become accustomed to, he turned, striding off up towards the peak of the mountain. Apollo and Nicos were alone.

Apollo gave a flick of his hand, and an elegant carved throne of gold and white marble appeared, into which he flopped. Another ornate throne appeared opposite, though it would be better described as a gilded chair. Nicos knew it was meant for him, but instead, he chose to sit himself on the ground. He watched, slightly transfixed, at how the light danced around Apollo; every beam caught the cut of his muscles perfectly. It caught him by surprise when he saw the God of Light watching him with a disarming smile.

Still, neither one said anything. Nicos looked over his shoulder in the direction Chiron had gone, wondering for a moment if he should go after him. He knew he couldn't really; Chiron always went to the peak of Mount Pelion alone.

"You look so much like her," Apollo's gentle, musical voice lifted the silence. "Your mother, I mean. She was one of wild beauty."

Nicos looked up from the grass he had been staring at to listen. Apollo spoke with such softness and admiration for the woman he never knew.

"I didn't know her as long as my sister, but in the time, I did... She was remarkable. Circe never wanted to be bound in games of gods, and she had magic enough to keep us all at bay. People say she is the most powerful witch that ever lived, and I believe it... until you, that is."

"I am not a witch," Nicos answered in surprise.

Apollo laughed and said, "Of course you are. Sure, you have gifts from divine blood, but you are a thousand times your mother's son. That makes you a witch. Don't be ashamed of it, for a name carries power."

The title of *witch* felt strange to Nicos, he had never considered it before. He had been raised as a hunter of Artemis, that is who he was and had always been until the day Artemis revealed his parentage. Then he was Nicos, the Son of Circe, and now he was to be titled as *witch*. Again, through the decisions of others, he felt as though his life was not his own. Apollo sensed the change in the young man before him and moved delicately from his throne to the ground before Nicos and draped his arm around him.

"Have I upset you?"

"No… not directly," Nicos answered. "It's just that everyone seems to tell me who I am… and I have no say. Funny really. I am a child outside of fate, and yet, I seem to tie in to everyone else's without much say." He was on his feet now, pacing.

"That I will not deny. You are tied to so many —well everyone —that must be an incredible burden." Apollo stood and placed his hands on Nicos' shoulders. "However, darling boy, no one can tell you who you are, you are whoever *you* choose to be… Just know that, when you name yourself, power comes with it."

Nicos looked up into the bright eyes of Apollo, searching them for any deception, but he was met with nothing but pure unfiltered truth. Nothing was said after that. Nicos went to freshen up in the cool water of the stream, his head whirring with the revelations of the day. The familiar tingle of a new magic began forming at the edges of his mind.

Apollo, in the meantime, returned to sit on his ornate throne to put himself in to a trance; his eyes turned a brilliant, bright gold. Nicos moved around him nervously at first, worried he may disturb him, but soon was going about his daily routine, as nothing seemed to distract Apollo from whatever it was, he was doing.

The sky had turned to the colours of early evening before Chiron returned. Nicos had a rabbit stew bubbling over a fire as he waved in greeting to the centaur. Apollo still sat in a trance on his throne.

"How was your time with Apollo?" Chiron asked as he lowered himself next to Nicos.

"It was… interesting. I learnt some more of Circe, and he named me a witch," Nicos replied.

Chiron gave a half-smile and said, "You seem surprised."

Nicos glanced up at the centaur but said nothing; instead, he heaped stew into two wooden bowls and handed one to his friend. They ate quietly together, occasionally Chiron would remark on the delightfulness of the stew, saying perhaps after all this is dealt with, Nicos might be a cook. Nicos laughed so hard he spat chunks of rabbit out.

"Lovely," Apollo said, raising his eyebrows at the sight.

This, of course, made the centaur and Nicos laugh harder. Apollo couldn't keep from letting out a bright musical laugh. Then, as quickly as the light-hearted moment had come, it left, as Apollo looked to Chiron with a solemn expression. With a heavy sigh, Chiron handed his empty bowl back to Nicos and got to his feet, and the pair took themselves away.

Nicos wanted to protest, after all, did this not concern him? Instead, he cleared away the dinner things, trusting that Chiron would tell him all when he needed to know. Besides, there was something else on his mind —the magic that had been niggling at him since Apollo's arrival.

He sat cross-legged by the stream and focused in on the sensation; it was like trying to catch sand. Most of it was clear as day, he could almost taste it, but there was something else that was eluding him.

Come on! Come on… I almost have you.

His hand stretched out in front of him, grasping at the air, but still he couldn't quite reach whatever it was. With a frustrated sigh, he let go of the feeling, knowing it would reveal itself at the right moment. He was quite surprised to see both Chiron and Apollo looking at him.

"You were working something magic, young one?" Apollo asked.

"Yes… how did you know?" Nicos replied.

"You have the same look as your mother," he smiled back warmly. Nicos was still caught by surprise at how moved he was at the warmth and affection Apollo held for the woman he had never known. Something like pride filled his heart, thinking that he shared this look with Circe.

"We have discussed much, Nicos. It is time we tell you all we have seen," Apollo said firmly.

Everything suddenly seemed very urgent.

"I have consulted the heavens," Chiron said, "and they are divided, meaning that those in Olympus have taken sides and the war is afoot. How many stands with us is yet unclear. As you know, anything that is bound to you becomes… changeable and hard to fix. After consulting with Apollo, I think it is safe to say Poseidon will at least not be in favour of Zeus. So, as far as we can see, the seas will be safe for you to cross. Artemis will obvi…"

"Cross the seas?" Nicos interrupted.

"Yes. Ah, I see. Well, I shall explain that first. I think, with the help of Apollo, I have deciphered your dream. We believe they are places you are meant to go in order to create, learn or… something. What you need from each place is unclear to us. I believe it is tied to your witchcraft." Chiron took in the face of Nicos; he suddenly seemed even younger than he had when they had met all those months ago. Apollo pulled three goblets out of the air and offered one filled with a sweet red wine to Nicos, who took it without looking at him.

"Your dreams, rather visions, are a map. Cerberus is the guardian of the gates to Hades, so you must need something that can only be found in the underworld. That much is easy, but I struggled with some of the others; with Apollo's help I think we have solved them. You see, they point to three women… three witches. Some might argue they would be as powerful as your mother. I knew of one straight away. The woman calling for Odysseus is the witch Calypso, cursed to never leave the island of Ogygia as a punishment for fighting on the side of the Titans in the great Titanomachy. Then it took me a while to work out who was next —the children's bones —but Apollo reminded me of the witch Lamia."

"A terrible story, really," Apollo muttered.

Chiron continued, "Lamia is found in Libya, where she was once Queen. The last escaped me because I had long forgotten about her and assumed she had died. She was married to one of my heroes before she killed their children and fled on a golden chariot pulled by dragons. That hero was Jason, and she was…"

"Medea," Nicos finished. There wasn't a person alive in Greece who didn't know the tale of the cruel witch, Medea.

"Yes. Finding her may prove difficult, but it seems she still lives, so find her you must," Chiron added sourly.

"Finally," Apollo took over, "is the island. I have no doubt that it is Aeaea, and the voice calling you is Circe. She is calling you home."

"Right," Nicos said softly.

He was trying to find better words to answer all he had been told, but that was all he could muster. Now he knew what his dream meant and that his journey to Pelion was only the beginning. Of course, it was! He knew that, really, but deep down there had been some childish hope that making it to Mount Pelion would be enough. There was enough time for the Olympians to forget all about him so he could return to the hunters' village, his real home. Back home to Thea and Korinna. But that childish hope was gone.

Chiron could see the weight of all that fell on Nicos' shoulders. He desperately wanted to lift it from him. It pained him to see it but he knew he hadn't finished.

"There is more…" Chiron said.

Nicos let out a sigh that expressed his exhaustion but gave a half-smile for the centaur to go on. Chiron spoke then of the division between the gods, saying again that it was hard to tell who was on his side, who might offer help, or, at the very least, who would not get in his way. Instead, he spoke firmly about who would be with Zeus. Hera, Ares, and Athena. They would undoubtedly be against him, so should avoid anything and anyone linked to them. Apollo spoke about how best to stay out of sight of Zeus; he was protected here on Pelion, but in time, Zeus would force Chiron's hand. Nicos didn't want to risk his friend's home or, indeed, his life.

The moon hung full and bright in the night sky. Nicos must have fallen asleep at some point, as he half woke to the feeling of Apollo's strong arms carrying him to bed. He felt the soft touch of the god's fingers brushing his hair from his face.

"Sleep well, Son of Circe," Apollo whispered as he left the sleeping Nicos, drifting into a dreamless sleep.

17

The days that followed were filled with plotting and planning. Chiron repeated the people that Nicos needed to find, hoping it might spark an idea of what he may need to find and, naturally, help him remember. Hades, Calypso, Lamia, Madea, and finally the island of Aeaea. He would have to leave Mount Pelion soon, but just not yet. Apollo expressed concern, saying that the longer he stayed with Chiron, the more likely Zeus would turn his gaze here to find him, but where else could he go?

This was something Nicos had been thinking about for nearly a week. The magic he felt still whispered around him; he knew it was something that would help keep Apollo hidden, something to help stop Zeus seeing them.

All he knew so far was that on the night of the full moon, he had to place a crystal bowl filled with water somewhere to catch the moon's light. Then various plants and herbs revealed themselves to him, so he would cut, crush, and rip them as they desired. This was how his magic worked. Anything that was needed would appear in a dream or would hold a bright aura about it, and as he touched it, it would tell him how to use it. Still, there was something missing —a missing ingredient. Nicos felt like it was staring him in the face, but try as he might, he couldn't see it. Annoyed, he decided, with Chiron's permission, to practice his archery, not that he needed to.

He was picking up his quiver of arrows when he cut his finger on an arrowhead. Looking down at the blood slowly seeping out, dripping onto the grass, a spark flashed through his mind. The last thing needed for this spell. His blood.

It all connected, making perfect sense, as though he had always known it. Nicos grabbed the herbs he had cut and crushed and added it to the moon water, then he let three drops of his blood fall into the bowl. It hissed gently before turning a dangerous shade of red.

"Apollo! Apollo!" Nicos called excitedly.

Apollo, who had been sat in his golden-eyed trance — which Nicos had learnt Apollo called gazing —The God of prophecy would cast his sight into possibilities of the future —came back to reality and hurried over to the excited Nicos.

"What is it? Are you hurt?" Apollo noticed the cut on his finger.

"I know how to keep you hidden," Nicos smiled. "I feel stupid; it took me so long, but I have it! My blood was the last piece. You see, you and Chiron say time and again that those who are with me are hard to see, invisible to the eyes of prophecy and gods, right?"

Apollo nodded, trying to keep up.

"Well," Nicos ploughed on, "what if you always had it on you —my blood and some other things to help boost its protection? My life essence but boosted. Zeus wouldn't be able to see you unless you were in front of him."

"It might work," Apollo said.

"It will work! I know my magic, Apollo, I know exactly what every potion I create does. This will keep you safe! A witch knows their work," Nicos reassured.

Apollo smiled, "So... you are a witch?"

"I am," Nicos said proudly as his cheeks flushed pink. For the first time, he felt he had chosen who he was, and he felt powerful. It was true what Apollo had said, knowing who you are and naming it gives you power.

Apollo looked down at the bowl of red liquid. He pressed his thumb and index finger together on both hands and brought them together. Slowly, as he pulled them apart, a clear crystal vial formed, about an inch long, with a small stopper attached to a thin chain of pure gold. Apollo removed the stopper and passed the vial to Nicos. Nicos filled it with the potion. The young witch looked at it with pride as he watched Apollo put the stopper back and seal it with a flash of light. Carefully, the God of Light lifted the chain over his head, feeling the crystal vial rest in the middle of his chest. It looked striking against his skin.

"Thank you," Apollo said with great humility.

"We should make one for Artemis too! Perhaps even a few more... just in case there are others that stand with us." Nicos said hopefully.

Apollo agreed and fashioned more of the crystal vials that Nicos filled before placing them in a leather pouch. They went on filling them until the potion was all gone and the pouch felt pleasantly weighty. Nicos instructed Apollo that the vial must be on them at all times to stay hidden from Zeus' visions, or indeed, anyone who may be using visions to track him or others.

With the newfound protection, Apollo informed the centaur and the witch that he was going to leave them for a while to find Artemis and then ready a boat for Nicos. Before anyone could protest or ask questions, Apollo had turned into the air.

The short week that followed almost felt similar to when Nicos had first arrived on Pelion. He and Chiron moved alongside each other easily, talking about the places and people he was set to find. Chiron told more about each of the witches —at least the bits he knew. The centaur's knowledge of Calypso seemed limited, saying that she had fallen in love with Odysseus and that Athena and Zeus had forced her to let him go. Lamia, tormented by Hera, had been transformed into a monster, though again he couldn't recall what Lamia's offence had been. However, his knowledge of Medea was vast, but it felt jaded, perhaps because Jason had been one of his students and, from what Nicos could gather, his favourite student. Nicos knew better than anyone not to entirely believe the version of a person from a story, but let it serve as a guide. Although stories are founded in truth, he knew women were rarely painted well.

The thought of facing other witches filled Nicos with excitement that was tempered by fear. He had never met another witch in his life. Now he was about to set out and face three of Greece's most dangerous. On top of this, he was also about to sail across the seas in a boat, something that felt completely alien to him. Nicos was a child of the forest, not of the seas. At least he could swim well, and it would stand to reason that as he was a child of Circe, he must have some sea nymph in him to draw on if the need arose. After all, Circe's mother, his grandmother, Perse, was the sea nymph who married the sun. The sea too was Poseidon's realm, and Nicos knew that he didn't stand with Zeus, which he hoped meant, at the very least, Poseidon wouldn't deliberately try to drown him.

A month passed, then another, and still Apollo hadn't returned. Nicos worried that perhaps he had failed, his magic hadn't protected him, and Zeus had sent a lightning bolt hurtling through the skies, erasing the God of Light, Music, and Prophecy from the earth. Chiron had reassured Nicos numerous times that Apollo was fine, saying they would have known if anything had happened to him. The death of a god would not go unheard, even up at the top of the mountain.

Late one night, as the centaur and Nicos readied themselves for bed, a deep rumbling echoed across the sky. Chiron looked at the young man beside him as lightning started to streak down repeatedly, seemingly in the same place. As if in response, the ground beneath them started to shake, softly at first, then it built to a crescendo, rougher, and harder until it felt as though something was trying to pull the mountain itself down. Nicos watched birds flee from trees as they fell, and then boulders and rocks tumbled, cascading down the mountain. On it went, the lightning and the earthquake. It seemed to go on for hours, until one last explosive bolt of lightning lit up the sky and one last deep, rumbling tremor shook the earth.

Then the sky and the earth were quiet —so quiet it sent a chill up the spine. It felt like the world was holding its breath. In the distance the glow of fires flickered, and Nicos could swear the screams and cries of the nearest town drifted in on the wind. His breath caught in his throat. Then, without warning, forks of ice-white lightning tore across the whole of the Grecian sky, etching onto the black night like a spiderweb. Chiron placed a strong hand on Nicos' shoulder, confirming what he already knew. This was Zeus. His fury on full display.

18

Silver moonlight bounced off the calm ocean as gentle waves kissed the sandy shore. Zeus stood facing the dark water, a serious look set on his face. He stood, working up the courage to swallow his pride and summon his brother Poseidon to meet with him. How could he say no when Zeus had come to meet him on the edge of his domain?

"Poseidon," Zeus called out to the sea. "Brother, will you come and speak with me?"

The King of Olympus stood there waiting on the white sand for several minutes before the figure of Poseidon rose out of the water before him, his dark skin shimmering in the light of the moon, golden trident in hand. He gave no answer to his brother as he stepped out of the water onto the white sand, locking eyes with him. They stood a few feet apart from one another, waiting to see who would speak first.

Selene, on her chariot, had pulled the moon further over the night sky before finally Zeus' thick voice split the uncomfortable silence.

"It is good to see you, brother."

"Don't lie," Poseidon answered back coldly.

"You forget yourself, Poseidon! Were you not my brother, I would…"

"Kill me? As you tried to Apollo?" Poseidon cut in, the venom in his voice palpable. "How is my nephew? I hear you are struggling to find him." A smile teased the Sea God's lips.

Zeus swallowed hard.

"You have called me here for what exactly, *dear* brother?"

"I need to know you are with me, not against me," Zeus answered, fighting to sound controlled. "It seems that the Olympian war has begun, and sides are being taken. I know you don't like my new decrees, but…"

Poseidon let out a laugh that sounded like waves crashing mercilessly against the rocks. It was a laugh as cold as the darkest depths of the ocean. Zeus' rage was building, and lightning crackled at his fingers. Poseidon saw this, so tightened his grip on his trident, and the waves behind him, on the once calm sea, began to kiss the shore a little harder.

"I will not stand with you. You see, Zeus, I think it is you who forgets yourself. You have forgotten what it is to be a fair and righteous king. Now you rule out of fear and wounded pride. You rule as our father Kronos once did. You think Circe's child has brought this war, but you forget that the Fates said it was inevitable. You are its cause. Perhaps it is time for a new king." Poseidon's stance changed into one ready for attack. It confused him then when Zeus laughed.

"You think that king, is you?"

Poseidon was annoyed now, "It could have been me when we drew those lots. Do you forget that it was chance when Hades, you, and I drew straws to see who would win dominion over what?"

"Chance?" Zeus laughed harder. "Please, little brother, I fixed the straws. Do you really think I, who cuckolded and dethroned Kronos, wouldn't fix the outcome of who would rule the heavens? You are stupid!"

Poseidon screamed, and the sea behind him raged in response.

"I came to see with whom you stand, and now I know," said Zeus. He raised his hand to the sky and brought it down in a strong sweep as lightning screamed through the air, striking repeatedly the spot where Poseidon had stood just a moment ago.

Poseidon had seen it coming, and before Zeus' arm had finished its journey, he had dived into the sea. Zeus hadn't even noticed he had missed it until he saw the sand turned to erupted glass and nothing else. A roar ripped from the King of the Olympians and shook the sky with thunder as he flung bolt after bolt towards the sea. Poseidon was borne up on a mighty wave, bellowing insults to the god on the sand.

"You cannot harm me here on the ocean, *brother!*" he taunted. "But you forget that I am the God of Earthquakes. I will shake all of Greece to the floor until you swear to leave me alone!"

With that, the beach beneath Zeus began to tremble, softly at first, as he kept throwing bolts of lightning at his defiant brother. Poseidon sent fierce waves towards the beach, covering the sand with the salty blanket of the sea, forcing Zeus to retreat higher up onto the land behind. The ground shook harder now, threatening to open below Zeus' feet and swallow him down to Hades. He could hear the people of the nearby town screaming as buildings gave way to Poseidon's earth-shaking.

As Zeus readied another bolt to launch at his brother, a hand caught him by the wrist.

"Enough!" It was Athena. "Father, enough."

Zeus let the lightning disappear, his hand still raised.

"Poseidon, stop this. You will destroy all of Greece with your pride, both of you." Athena's voice carried like a steady ship on the air to the Sea God's ear. The ground started to steady, and the waves that had drowned the beach began to subside. Poseidon lowered himself to the sand once more, and pointed his trident threateningly at Zeus, daring him to come closer.

"If you ever try to eradicate me again, Zeus, I swear on the Styx, I will bring all of Greece to its end!" Poseidon promised as he disappeared into the sea. The last of the waves died down, and the sea returned to the calm, glassy stillness of when the night began.

Zeus screamed in fury, sending lightning rippling across the night sky.

19

A message came to Mount Pelion the morning after the sky had been fractured by lightning. A white raven cawed as it made its decent from the sky towards Nicos, who held out his arm for it. This was Apollo's herald. Carefully, Nicos unfastened a small piece of parchment from the bird's leg. As soon as it was unfastened, the white raven took off back to his master.

Dearest Nicos,

The time has come for you to leave Pelion. I have much to tell you, but it is best we meet elsewhere, as I believe Zeus will be calling on Chiron soon. It is more to do with myself than you, but still, it is best you are gone so Chiron can erase any evidence of your existence. Meet me on the outskirts of Iolkos. You will find us in the pasture of dianthus flowers.

Your loyal friend,
Apollo.

Nicos read the message several times. Every time he reread the words; a different emotion would cascade through his body like a waterfall. First, he felt relief —relief that

Apollo was okay and that his magic had worked. Then came fear at the idea of Zeus coming here to the mountain, muddled with sadness for his friend's safety and also that his time here was coming to an end. From the day he had arrived, Nicos knew he would one day have to leave. Now that time had come, more abruptly than he had imagined.

Without much talk, Chiron readied a bag of dried meat and fruit, tucking in some herbs found only on the mountain. Nicos, on the other hand, gathered up his kopis and Korinna's bronze bone-handled dagger that he hadn't touched since he had arrived. As he fixed the blade about his waist, he noted it felt heavier. Perhaps, he thought, when you live without the need for a weapon, when you lift it again, you feel the weight of its danger.

It didn't take long for the pair to erase any sign of Nicos ever having been with Chiron. A whole year and a half gone; now it only lived in their memories. Except, that is, for the potions that Chiron had learnt from his student. With his bag of food over his shoulder, blades at his waist, bow, and quiver fixed to his back, Nicos turned to face his friend. He had thought saying goodbye to Thea and the hunters would be the hardest goodbye he would ever say, but now he was choking on the words that stuck in his throat.

"My dear Nicos, of all the heroes I have known, you are by far the best of them all," Chiron said, his voice thick with emotion. "I am proud to have been a moment in your great epic."

"You are so much more than a moment, Chiron, you are my teacher, my friend." Nicos felt a tear trace down his cheek. The centaur wiped it away gently with his thumb.

"Shed no tears, sweet Son of Circe; this parting is not one of sadness but of pride." Chiron pulled Nicos into a tight embrace, his arms wrapping around where man became horse. When Nicos pulled away, he took a steady breath and looked up into the warm face of his friend.

"When Zeus comes..." Nicos started.

"I will face him," Chiron answered firmly. His voice betrayed some kind of knowing that Nicos could not understand. "Now be on your way, head straight to Iolkos."

"I need to fetch an old friend first, then I will head straight there." Nicos turned to start his decent.

"Remember, Nicos, you are outside of fate, but all are linked to you. Do what you think is right, trust your heart, and decide for yourself." Chiron called after him as he disappeared through the trees.

***

It was late afternoon when Nicos stood at the end of a dirt road leading up to a lonely farmhouse. A smile spread across his face at the sight of it. He took off at a run to reach the home of Merope and Dimitrios. The stable out front still housed two old nags and a mule, and there, shining like polished obsidian, stood Theron. When the horse saw his old friend, it whinnied and trotted out to meet Nicos. They pressed their heads together in greeting.

"Hello, my friend. You didn't think I had forgotten about you, did you?"

Nicos marvelled at how well the horse looked. Clearly, Dimitrios had taken good care of the stallion. His muscles were strong and his coat as smooth as silk; so too, it seemed, were the two other older horses. Nicos' heart filled, taking it as a sure sign that the old couple had been left alone for all this time. Dimitrios had come to the doorway at the sound of the whinnies of Theron and was overcome with joy to see Nicos stood outside.

"By the gods! You have come back to us!" Dimitrios cheered as he cleared the distance between them in no time to pull Nicos into a tight embrace. "Come in, come in my lad! Merope!"

Dimitrios took him by the elbow and pulled him inside. There, Merope, who had been stood over a bubbling pot of what looked to be a vegetable stew, let out a squeak of delight and had her arms about him in seconds.

"How well you look, Nicos. So strong, perhaps a little thin still," Merope said in a motherly fashion as she slapped his stomach "Say you will stay with us for dinner?"

"If you will have me," Nicos smiled. He noticed the table was already set for three. "Though, if you have company already, I don't want to intrude."

"Nonsense." Dimitrios said as he set a fourth place. "There is a young man who has been with us since, well, nearly since you left us. He was looking for a place to stay, and in return, he has been aiding us on the farm. He has also been running the horses, keeping Theron in shape and well groomed,"

"I must thank him then," Nicos answered as he took a jug of wine from Merope and set it on the table. He sat and poured out three goblets of the bright red wine. They told him how they had been blessed since Nicos had scared off the bandits. Their harvest was full, and for the first time in years, they got it all to the nearest market to sell, making a small fortune. This new man who had come after had also helped to fix parts of the house and stables, much to the delight of Dimitrios, who had exclaimed several times that Zeus must have rewarded them for their hospitality towards Nicos. This made Nicos laugh.

If only you knew how the God of all Gods really felt about me.

Merope began to serve up the steaming stew as the sound of footsteps came from outside.

"It smells good in here Merope," a familiar voice said. "Oh, we have company, hello."

Nicos stood to greet the stranger. Only, to his utter surprise, it was no stranger at all, it was…

"Zander?" Nicos' mouth dropped in surprise to see the handsome man of Athens here in the farmhouse. This was the man who had arrived just after him? How can that be? So many questions whirled around his head. It *had* been him then who he had seen as he set out all that time ago to Mount Pelion.

"Well, I never?!" Merope exclaimed. "You two know each other?"

"We met in Athens a year and some ago." Zander's face was lit up with a bright, dazzling smile. Nicos had forgotten how beautiful it was. His eyes too, he didn't remember them being so bright.

"It seems the Fates are binding you together," Dimitrios said as he took a spoonful of stew.

"So, it seems," said Zander as he took his place at the table.

Nicos was still in shock, it wasn't until Merope gave a little cough that he came back to his senses, and he sat too.

Dimitrios, Merope, and Zander talked of the day's chores, what had been done and what hadn't. The whole time his eyes kept flicking to look at Nicos, who found it hard not to look at the man he had left in Athens.

When the conversation turned to Nicos and where he had been, he wondered what to say. If it had just been Merope and Dimitrios, he was sure he would have told them everything — well, almost everything. He couldn't do that with Zander here, could he? He had never been one to lie, so all he said was, "I was studying under a wise teacher in Pelion, and now I am heading on to a new destination to continue my studies."

The night had come quickly, and, though he protested, Dimitrios convinced Nicos that he must stay the night as it was far too late to travel. As before, he had managed to get what little Nicos had brought with him into the room he had stayed in the time before. Nicos couldn't help but grin.

As he prepared himself for bed, the door opened, and Zander stepped in.

"You are sure you don't mind sharing the room with me?" Zander asked, and his smooth voice set something off in Nicos. "I really don't mind sleeping elsewhere."

"No, its fine. Unless you would rather?" Nicos said.

"I am quite happy to share a room with you, Nicos," Zander gave a wink.

Nicos turned to hide his blushing face.

The two men continued to ready themselves for bed. Nicos couldn't help watching Zander pull off his sweaty tunic, revealing his hairy, scarred chest. He bit his lip and forced his eyes away. When he turned around again, Zander was sitting on the bed, covered by a sheet of fabric.

"How are you here?" Nicos blurted out.

"I wondered when you would ask," Zander smiled.

So, the Athenian told him how he had left Athens the same afternoon Nicos had. He had been compelled, he had reasoned, to know more of the man he had met at Jocasta's the night before. It was hard for Nicos not to blush at the brazen compliment; after all, it is not everyone who declares that Eros had struck them so plainly upon meeting. Still, Nicos said nothing, letting Zander recount to him his journey to the farm of Merope and Dimitrios.

"I had hoped," Zander began, "that I might catch up to you on the road, seeing as you were only a few hours ahead of me. It never occurred to me that I didn't actually know where you were headed until much further along my way. But I knew the direction you had set, and so I went. I rode straight until the night drew in and it was too dark to continue. I slipped from the road and slept in a wooded part of the mountain. I was on my way again by first light, afraid to be caught out by any wolves or bears."

Nicos sat himself on the floor, his back leaning against the cool, smooth, stone wall. Zander offered for him to sit on the bed, but he declined and gestured for him to continue.

"Well, then came days of riding. I had no idea what I would say when I found you, but I just... I felt compelled to find you," Zander spoke so plainly it was quite disarming. "I enjoyed the journey, if truth be told; I heard incredible stories of a young man who stalked bandits astride a horse of Hades and a pack of wolves that foamed at the mouth."

Nicos laughed.

"What?"

"Nothing," Nicos answered quickly.

"Anyway, I must have been riding near a week when I came to the farmhouse. I had been told to be wary when heading in that direction as I passed through a village near the foot of Mount Pelion. The people warned of a divine being that controlled the birds themselves." It was Zander's turn to laugh. "I was exhausted and all but ready to give up. That is when I saw Dimitrios brushing your horse. I knew it to be yours instantly. Well, you know how kind and generous Merope and Dimitrios are, they took pity on me, seeing my torn tunic… how dirty I had become. They offered me food and a place to stay for the night. That night turned into a week, a month, and then a year, and I'm still here."

"Why?" Nicos asked.

"Isn't it obvious?" Zander genuinely looked a little embarrassed. "I have been waiting for you."

Nicos' face flushed a bright red; he was grateful for the low candlelight that prevented Zander seeing.

"I knew you would come back for Theron, and I enjoyed helping them out. They, too, knew you would return to them. Look, it is late; shall we talk more in the morning?"

"Okay," Nicos mumbled as he blew out the candles. Zander again offered the bed but didn't press the matter and lay back as Nicos settled himself on the ground. He listened as Zander's breath became slow and steady with sleep.

Nicos lay awake for some time. He found it hard to believe that anyone would follow a stranger after meeting only briefly, especially when on one of those times the other person had been quite drunk. Sure, there was an attraction to the man that felt animal and primal, but would he have done the same? Follow a stranger in the hopes of what? What did Zander expect of him now? If he didn't have to reach Iolkos, if he wasn't tied into a war between gods, would he go with Zander? It made him lightheaded.

Perhaps Eros really had struck Zander in the heart, and so here he was. Nicos couldn't deny the many times he had found himself with wandering thoughts about the Athenian whilst with Chiron. Not all of those thoughts had been improper; in fact, had he not wondered what it might have been between them if he could have stayed in Athens? All of this was not important now. He would be leaving tomorrow morning to meet with Apollo, leaving Zander behind again. He rolled over, ignoring the little burst of sadness that bubbled inside, and let sleep finally take him.

20

Nicos stirred as the morning sun danced across his face from the open window. He let out a small groan of satisfaction as he stretched on the floor, his eyes fluttering open. He looked over to see if Zander was awake, only to find him already gone. With a great effort, Nicos pulled himself to his feet and splashed his face with the water that sat in a wooden bowl. Zander must have brought it up some time earlier. After pulling on his forest green tunic, Nicos gathered up his things and glided down the stairs to see Merope alone in the kitchen.

"I hope you weren't planning on slipping away," she said with her back to Nicos as he stood at the foot of the stairs.

"I wouldn't dream of it." Nicos smiled and sat at the table just as Merope placed a bowl of fresh figs in front of him.

"Dimitrios will be back shortly. He went with Zander to fix something or other; then you can both be on your way." She sat beside him.

"Both?"

"Zander is going with you is he not?" Merope asked.

Nicos nearly choked on the fig he had bitten into. "Coming with me? No, he can't."

Merope looked at Nicos thoughtfully for a quiet moment. "He travelled all this way and waited for over a year just to be with you. Whatever it is you are off to do, he seems like a man to have by your side." She raised a hand to stop Nicos from interrupting. "I have lived a long time and seen many things. Zander has been struck on the order of Aphrodite, and I think, too, so have you. I see it in your eyes, though you fight to conceal it."

Nicos' cheeks flushed a gentle shade of pink.

"Merope, I cannot have him with me." Nicos took a deep breath before saying, "I am bound to the fates of the gods, where I must go… it's no place for… it's wrought with danger; no one is supposed to know anything; how then can I take him with me?"

The old woman nodded her head, seemingly acknowledging something she already knew.

"I knew that you were more than mortal." She took his hand in hers, squeezing it lovingly. "I think that it must be lonely to have no one you can trust. Zander is a good person with a kind heart. I know he will follow you, even if you asked him to stay. So why not tell him and let him decide?"

Nicos stood and kissed her on the cheek. There was something in the wisdom of the old lady he couldn't deny. He went out to find Theron to get him ready for the next leg of their journey, whilst Nicos turned over the idea of telling Zander.

"What do you think old friend? Should I tell him what I am, where I am headed, and for what end? Can he really feel that strongly for me in such a short time? Do I really feel the same for him? What do you think, Theron? Is Zander trustworthy?"

The horse whinnied and tapped his hoof in answer.

Behind him, Nicos could hear the hearty laughter of Dimitrios. He turned then to see the old man and Zander walking in step up the dirt road. Zander saw Nicos standing by Theron, and with a quick word to Dimitrios, he sprinted up to reach him.

"You were just going to go?" Zander made no effort to hide his disappointment. "You know I am coming with you!"

"Are you?" Nicos tried his best to sound standoffish.

Zander rolled his eyes. "You didn't think I would let you disappear again after all this time? I am aware I sound as though I have lost my senses, but Nicos, I feel like fate has wound you and me together."

"You think that, from a chance meeting and a drunken proposition?" Nicos was fighting hard to keep the smile that tugged at the corners of his mouth.

"Wha… you remember that?" Zander's face went crimson with embarrassment. It was the first time Nicos had ever seen the burly man look vulnerable.

"I wasn't drunk," Nicos answered letting the smile finally break. Dimitrios had caught up to them now, but giving them both a wave, he mumbled something and headed straight for the house.

"If you don't want…" Zander began, but Nicos cut him off.

"Zander… It is not so simple. If you come with me, then I have to tell you the truth of where I am headed, and I am not sure if I can. There are others whom it will affect, and I don't know you."

Zander furrowed his brow, "Are you in trouble?"

"No… and yes. If I am to trust you, will you swear on the Styx to never tell another living soul?" Nicos' voice was serious.

"I swear on the Styx; I will tell no other mortal of anything you tell me."

Nicos told Zander almost everything. Of the gods, the war, being beyond fate, his mother, and where he was headed next. All the while, Zander's face was fixed in concentration, he was taking it remarkably well. He left out the capability of his powers and who the witches were that he was meant to find; something told him to keep that to himself, instead, he just said he was a witch, simple and plain. When Zander asked who his father was, Nicos said nothing. After all, technically he didn't have a father.

"So, there it is. Do you really want to come with me?"

Zander put his strong hand on Nicos' shoulder and said, "When do we leave?"

"Within the hour," Nicos had in turn put his hand on the broad shoulder of the man in front of him.

Zander went to gather up the little he had brought with him from Athens, whilst Nicos readied the horses. Nicos felt an excitement bubble in his stomach. In telling Zander, he had gained a friend he had never expected, and it somehow made the danger that lay ahead less frightening. It confused him really. Here he was, a powerful witch, with divine gifts from two Olympians, as well as the teachings of the wisest centaur ever to have lived, topped off with the divine protection and guardianship of at least two gods; yet it was the company of a mortal that brought a feeling of safety and adventure. Nicos then pondered the question, was it Zander himself that made him feel this way, or could it have been any fellow Greek?

He, of course, knew the answer to this. There was something about Zander that excited him as much as it steadied him. The confidence of the man and how he so brazenly told of his feelings reassured him. He was honest.

The horses readied, he turned to see Merope coming towards him from the farmhouse. She carried a small bag in her hand, which Nicos knew to be filled with food.

"It's not much," she said, "But it will get you both through the next few days. I am glad you told him."

"So am I," Nicos replied.

"Trust and love Nicos; that is what gives us heart and reason to go on. Be safe and be smart, if the fate of the gods and Greece are in you, then I know we are all in good hands." Merope pulled him down to her, and she kissed him on the cheeks. She held him just that little bit longer. When they finally let go, their eyes blurry with held back tears, Dimitrios and Zander had joined them.

As Nicos embraced Dimitrios, Zander say his goodbyes to Merope. Then both men climbed up onto their horses and started off towards Iolkos. Nicos kept glancing back over his shoulder until the farmhouse disappeared from view, knowing that the old couple would have stood there watching until they were both out of sight.

It was pleasant to have someone to travel with. Nicos had never really gotten used to travelling alone; now, with Zander beside him, it made the journey go quicker. The road towards Iolkos was straight and easy; they hardly passed anyone. Zander had mentioned that many people were afraid that Zeus was to light up the sky again. The two horses kept a steady pace as the men got to know each other more —well, as much of each other as Nicos would share. Lying wasn't something

Nicos enjoyed, or even did well, so he had learnt to tell part truths. Thea had once told him human beings share too much of themselves, and all he would ever need to do is tell enough of the truth so anyone can fill in the rest as they wish.

So, when Zander spoke of his father being from an old family of Athens, Nicos said the little he knew of Circe and that he was raised by trusted guardians by the names of Thea and Korinna. When Zander said he grew up in the busy metropolis of Athens, Nicos said he grew up in a very tight village a short way from the city. Nicos realised the more he knew of Zander, the more he found the man attractive. Beyond the physical attraction came this new feeling that comes when you begin to see into the heart of someone.

The city of Iolkos was nearing ahead, and, using his gift of sight, he could see a field of dianthus flowers off to the left from the direction they were going. Nicos asked Theron to stop, and Zander, following him, did the same.

"I need to go to meet…" he hesitated, "my friends alone. I need to tell them of you, and I don't know how they will take it."

Zander gave a curt nod, "Don't fret on it. I'm not sure I am ready to meet a god yet anyway. Why don't I head on into the city and find us a room for the night?"

"Yes, alright," Nicos grinned, "I will see you soon then."

"You will," Zander smiled warmly.

21

Nicos rode a short while in the direction of the dianthus field. He chanced a look back once to see that Zander wasn't following, and he was relieved to see he was heading straight into Iolkos. A man of his word, it seemed. It eased Nicos, too, that Zander had been so understanding about why he couldn't come with him. Now it was time to set his focus on the task at hand. There was no denying that he was looking forward to seeing Artemis and Apollo again, but he knew that it came with more news of Zeus and the latest developments in the hunt for him.

The field of flowers was possibly the most beautiful thing Nicos had yet seen in his young life. He slipped down from Theron to marvel at the wonderous sea of pinks, purples, and reds that covered the ground. It was so inviting against the crisp blue of the sky. He noticed the field was empty, no Apollo or Artemis were yet present. Nicos didn't mind, in fact, he was a little relieved to be able to enjoy the beauty alone for just a moment. Kneeling down to get a closer look at the frilled petals, Nicos noticed the sweet scent that filled his nose. Gently, he ran a finger over the petals, relishing their delicate silky feel on his fingertips.

"They are beautiful, aren't they?" came a soft voice.

"Incredibly so," Nicos replied without looking. It took a moment for him to realise that the voice that had spoken didn't belong to Artemis or Apollo. His body tensed, and his right hand deftly moved to the hilt of his sword. With a steadying breath, he stood slowly, his grip tightening.

"I mean you no harm, Nicos, Son of Circe. I am Demeter. I have been waiting for you," she said. "I thought you would have arrived yesterday, but it seems you were delayed?"

Nicos turned then to face the God of Harvest, his hand still tight around his sword. She looked harmless enough, he thought, but he knew who this was. This was the immortal who nearly destroyed the earth in search of her daughter, even now, she can bring on bad harvests and harsh winters. The flowers all seemed to be brighter at her feet, as though she stood on a soft pink halo. Her autumn amber eyes were locked on Nicos.

"Demeter," Nicos inclined his head in greeting, "forgive me, I had to fetch my horse, and my friends who cared for him had me stay the night."

"I understand. You can relax your grip on your sword, I won't harm you." Demeter smiled.

"I am sure you are aware that I am not well loved amongst your kind." Nicos answered, sounding a lot stronger than he felt. His eyes scanned the surrounding area quickly to see if there was any sign of Apollo. Perhaps he had been caught, or worse. What if Demeter was here to keep him in place until Zeus was ready to strike? Demeter walked towards him with effortless grace.

"You are right to be cautious, but this might help convince you I am not a threat." Demeter held out her right arm, and there, around her wrist, was a small crystal vial of red liquid fixed on an intricate gold and green bracelet.

"My potion?" Nicos whispered as his grip loosened on his sword.

"Given to me by Apollo. I was asked to guard the field of dianthus flowers until you arrived. I have sent for them, and they will be with us shortly, I am sure," Demeter explained.

"Is it just you?"

"No. Of course there are the twins, myself, Aphrodite, and her husband…" Demeter listed.

"Hephaestus?" Nicos added.

"Precisely."

"Poseidon?" He asked quietly.

"That I don't know… I think Artemis will know more of that." Demeter turned to raise her hands. The ground shook a little as six chairs of earth and flowers began to form in a close circle. All seemed to be of equal height, except one that sat slightly shorter than the rest; it seemed plain, although it was still beautiful, covered in the pink shades of the dianthus. This seat, Nicos knew, was meant for him. It annoyed him that, even in this moment, the gods who needed him saw him as lesser. Demeter seemed unaware as she now raised a table of stones in the centre, and on top appeared a cornucopia with food spilling, covering the surface. Goblets of gold came next, each with a divine emblem engraved, except one silver chalice that, again, seemed meant for Nicos.

"Just in time," said Demeter as she turned to see Apollo, Artemis, Aphrodite, and Hephaestus appear out of the air, gliding towards them in silent splendour.

Apollo was first to reach Nicos. He pulled him into a tight, warm embrace; the warmth of his skin enveloped him, and for that fleeting second, he felt so safe. The coolness of the air came as a surprise when Apollo let go as he moved aside to greet Demeter. Artemis reached him then and placed a cool, firm hand on his shoulder.

"You look well. It is so good to see you again, Nicos," Artemis' voice rippled with pride.

"You too," Nicos said, looking up at her smiling.

Then she, too, stepped past him, and he was left looking up at the Goddess of Love and the God of Fire. Nicos marvelled at the beauty that he now realised no artist, poet, or scholar had been able to truly capture. The soft pink dress she wore clung delicately to her body, as though it never wanted to let her go. Her eyes were like green pools he would have gotten lost in had Hephaestus not spoken to him.

"So, you are the Son of Circe." the god's voice was deep and rich, like it came from the depths of the mountains themselves.

"That would be me," Nicos pulled his gaze to look into his smoky grey eyes. By Olympian standards, Hephaestus was considered ugly because of his scar and hunched back, but not to Nicos; to him Hephaestus's face was rugged and handsome.

"You are taller than I expected," Hephaestus remarked, more to himself than anyone else. Aphrodite gave a heartbreaking smile as she took her husband by the arm and steered him into the gathering of gods. Nicos turned and watched silently as they all spoke amongst themselves, seemingly forgetting he was there. He was glad for that, for he could take a minute to let his head catch up with what was happening. As he observed them, the witch among immortals, he noticed each had on them a crystal vial holding his magic.

Aphrodite's was fixed into the middle of a silver dolphin broach; Hephaestus had his fixed into a wrought iron arm band that was tightly fixed on his left bicep; and Artemis wore hers in between the two crescent moons of her circlet atop her head.

"Shall we all be seated then? After all, there is much we need to catch up on, I am sure." Apollo's musical voice rang out.

Each god made their way to sit on the flowered earth thrones, leaving the smallest free. Demeter gestured for Nicos to take his place there, her intention was friendly, but it sent a prickle of irritation down the back of his neck.

"Is something wrong?" Demeter looked genuinely perplexed at the mortal's refusal.

"Yes, there is." Artemis answered for him. "Why is his seat smaller than ours?"

"Is it not proper? We are still Olympians, even if we have broken from Zeus." Demeter asked in innocent confusion.

"Nicos is a witch in whom all of us have put our trust. If that does not make him our equal, then perhaps we are as bad as our father," Artemis said in an icy tone.

Demeter said nothing but raised his throne to the height of all the others. Nicos knew then, in that moment, that he was more than their equal. They needed him more than he knew; the great Olympians needed his witchery to take on their father. It was daunting, but oddly thrilling. He gained a sense of assuredness that made him want to be heard, and he vowed to himself that, in the presence of these gods, he would be.

"Thank you," Nicos said as he sat down, "So where do we begin?"

"Firstly, thanks are in order," Apollo began, "your magic has kept its promise. We cannot be seen by any being who is gifted with sight. Introductions are perhaps not needed now, but everyone here has taken your side against Zeus."

"Hold on!" Nicos interrupted. "It is Zeus who is against me. I understood your war was inevitable, my birth merely sped up the occurrence. Be clear on why you are against him, beyond my desire. I am to affect the outcome, yes, but how that is to be done, I do not know."

Nicos' boldness caught everyone by surprise, himself included.

"We are at war with Zeus because he has lost sight of much," Aphrodite said. "He broke the Olympian treaty by putting restrictions on us all that affect our duties as Gods of Greece…"

"And our pleasures too," Apollo added.

"Punishing your mother, as he did, was born out of fear, with no chance of reasoning. So much of his rulings now are based in that same fear." Demeter said softly.

"You are the spark, dear Nicos, and we are to defend and aid you, so that when the time comes, you can do as you must," Artemis said.

"Tell me then, what is the news of Zeus?" Nicos asked, noticing, too, that the silver goblet had now also been made gold.

"He is consumed with fear and a hunger for maintaining power. Ares has his favoured war mongers and kings on high alert for any sign of you, Dionysus's maenads have been given permission to spread from Thebes in the hunt for Circe's son," Artemis said methodically.

Nicos swallowed hard. It confirmed something he already knew —nowhere was safe.

Artemis continued, "We as a collective have been doing all we can to throw false leads, to try and lead Zeus in the wrong direction. The closest he has been to you since this all began was two nights ago when he faced Poseidon."

"When the sky was torn apart by lightning?"

"Yes. Zeus attacked Poseidon when he refused to join him. If Athena hadn't stepped in, I think half of Greece would have been destroyed," said Apollo.

"So, is Poseidon with us?"

"He is… we think," Apollo answered, "It is our opinion that Poseidon will be firmly with us when he meets you."

Nicos looked at Apollo in surprise.

"Poseidon is a proud God, not unlike Zeus," Demeter said now in her calm, grounded voice. "If you were to summon him, speak directly with him, and ask a favour of him, then he will stand with you."

"What favour would I need of him?" Nicos asked a little perplexed.

"Poseidon needs to feel that you are not all powerful, as Zeus believes, and by asking for his aid, it will show that you value the need for us Olympians," Demeter continued. "Apollo has sought out a modest boat that will carry you across the seas, but obviously we can't hire a crew, as it will raise too many questions…"

"At first I thought to capture the winds in the sail so they might steer you on," Apollo interrupted, "but then Demeter suggested this is where we can sway Poseidon. As king of the sea, he could command the waves to carry you anywhere you wanted."

A long moment of silence fell between them all as Nicos' mind worked to process the new information. He had to meet with Poseidon and ask for his help, which in turn would secure the gods allegiance. It sounded so convoluted, but then again, this was part of the problem with Olympians, nothing was ever simple.

"I shall meet with him first thing tomorrow, then," said Nicos.

Then, between Artemis and Apollo, Nicos was told he would find his boat in the port of Pagasae under the care of a trusted ally of Artemis, who went by the name of Alyosha. Demeter told him more about how to best win over Poseidon, tradition, and ritual. It was so much to absorb. At some point, Nicos had noticed how far the sun had travelled across the sky. He knew that the time was coming to tell them about Zander. He had just worked up the courage to say something when Artemis spoke, "There is something else I must tell you, but it won't be easy to hear."

Nicos' eyes flicked up to look straight into her yellow eagle eyes, a sudden coldness bubbled in his stomach.

"At the last summoning, I threatened to shoot Zeus in defence of Apollo, and in response to all that was said between us, he took revenge. He went after my hunters."

It felt as though the world had been pulled out from under him.

"I had just reached the village in time to tell Thea that they should move on when Zeus appeared and threw thunderbolts blindly in all directions, killing them all, leaving nothing of the settlement unharmed. I still hear their screams as they were slaughtered."

Nicos could barely breathe as tears fell silently down his face. Everyone who had ever raised him, everyone who loved him, was gone. Erased in a gods fit of anger. He had always hoped that he might see them again. His heart was breaking, and a pain that he had never known clawed at his chest.

"Nicos, I am so sorry I couldn't save them all. I never imagined my father would..." She was kneeling before him now, with her hands on his knees. "Can you forgive me?"

"I do not blame you," Nicos choked out, his lungs burning, holding back the trapped scream that was fighting to get out. He noticed then that Artemis' eyes were filled with tears, threatening to spill, as she had loved them more than he knew.

"I did manage to save one of them. She wants to come with you if you will allow it."

"Who...?" Nicos whispered.

Artemis took his hand and pulled him to his feet. She turned him to face outside the circle, and, with a hunter's whistle, Thea appeared a short distance away in the flowers. Nicos broke out into a run to cover the short distance and flung his arms around her. Thea, in turn, pulled Nicos as close to her as she could, both of them letting the pain of loss flow freely. It's hard to say how long they stayed locked together, but when the tears slowed and their breathing levelled, the colours of dusk painted the sky.

"Today has been a long one for you, sweet Nicos, and I think it is time to send you on your way," Apollo said, wiping the last few tears from his face.

All the gods had gathered around them now.

"I am working on something for each of you. Something that will keep you safe in the final meeting between Zeus,"

Hephaestus said for the first time since they met. "I needed to meet you first, to know you, so I can craft the perfect piece that will suit only you and, of course, Thea."

"Thank you," Nicos said, "There is one more thing I need to say before you all go."

Each immortal looked at one another, unsure of what was left to be said.

"I have brought a mortal into our confidence." Nicos raised his voice over the muttered disproval and said, "His name is Zander, and I have told as much as I could without betraying your confidence or sharing too much of mine. He is a good man and will be a faithful ally to me."

"How did you meet?" Artemis asked in a prickled manor.

"What have you said?" Demeter questioned, a trace of panic in her voice.

"Why would you do this?" Apollo sounded angry.

"He loves him," Aphrodite said plainly as she stared into Nicos' soul. "You protest it, but I know the beginnings of love, I have seen it in all. All we need to know is, do you trust him?"

"Yes," Nicos answered simply. It was the easiest question he had been asked in a long time.

"Then there is no more to be said. Apollo, give me a crystal."

Apollo reached into the pouch at his waist and placed the blood-red liquid-filled crystal into her palm. She held it towards Hephaestus, who placed his hand over it. Bright light spilled between their pressed palms for a fleeting second, and then Hephaestus moved his hand away to reveal, in Aphrodite's palm, a ring of rose gold and fixed like a gem into it was the vial.

"Give this to him so he may be safe, if ever you are parted." Aphrodite couldn't keep the smile from her face. She kissed Nicos' cheek, turned to link arms with her husband, and they were gone.

Demeter gave a nod of her head, vanished the thrones and table, and was gone. Then it was just the four of them: Artemis, Apollo, Thea, and Nicos.

"Thank you for bringing me back to my son." Thea's voice was tired with grief as Artemis wrapped her arms around her friend.

"I am sorry I couldn't give you more."

"Nicos, love can blind us, be cautious a little with this man," said Apollo. He almost sounded fatherly, Nicos thought. "If you say he is a good man, then we will trust you."

"He is, Apollo, I know it."

Apollo hugged his friend tightly, and then he gave a little wave and turned into the air.

"Thank you for saving her, Artemis. Please know you couldn't have done more." Nicos whispered into the goddess' ear as he pulled her into a rigid embrace. The words softened her, and she hugged him back. At some point, she was gone.

Thea and Nicos still hadn't really said anything to each other. They didn't need to, not yet. Nicos took Thea by the hand, and they walked towards Theron, only to see that Thea wasn't the only survivor of Zeus' massacre. Zephyra stood strong beside her old friend.

"So…" Thea said, in that tone only a mother can hold, as she pulled herself up on her horse. Nicos felt his hair tingle on the back of his neck, as though he were five again and had been caught doing something he shouldn't. "Who is this, Zander?"

22

Zander watched as Nicos rode off in the opposite direction. When he was sure that he was out of sight, he turned his horse around and rode the other way. He rode fast and hard towards the thick forest that grew up a few miles away. His heart was pounding in his chest, threatening to break out through his ribs. When he was deep enough amongst the trees and sure no passersby could spy him, he dismounted and tied his horse to a tree. Then, walking a little away from the horse, Zander reached into his pocket to pull out a silver owl broach.

"My great Goddess Athena, I ask you to come forth, bless me with your presence," Zander spoke into the thick forest air.

The trees around gave a creaking groan and moved apart, creating a perfect grassy circle, upon which now stood the grey-eyed God, Athena. She stood resplendent with the sun, lighting her up from behind. Zander dropped to his knee and lowered his head until her long, cold fingers lifted him by the chin. Even with her godhood dimmed, it still stung his eyes to look upon the warrior goddess.

"Do you have some news?" asked Athena.

"Yes, great Athena," Zander said as he got to his feet at the indication of the goddess. "He returned to the house exactly as I told you he would. Nicos is his name, and he has been studying under the guise of a teacher near Pelion."

Athena gave a knowing nod, as though Zander had confirmed something she had long been suspecting.

"I have won his trust."

"How?" asked Athena.

"I told him that Eros struck my heart on our first meeting. No being is impervious to the thrill of being desired," Zander answered. He left out, of course, that he actually did have feelings for Nicos; try as he might to temper them from being real.

"Love… such a silly thing to blind so many. Aphrodite is a dangerous god, though many think her frivolous." Athena spoke more to herself than Zander, though he took it as approval for his method.

"He meets now with Apollo and Artemis in a place near Iolkos; then we are to sail in the hunt of a witch," said Zander.

"What witch?" Athena's voice suddenly sharp, so sharp it made Zander start.

"I am not sure; he wouldn't say who or where." Zander swallowed hard; he knew this was not the answer Athena wanted.

Athena clenched her fists. "You must find out and tell me as soon as you can. What more do you know?"

"I know not as much as you may wish…yet. I know we are to find three great witches of Greece; for what purpose I don't know. There is much they haven't shared, but they will… in time." Zander spoke quickly, summoning all the courage he had in him. "I have served you well all my life, have I not great Athena?"

She nodded.

"Then trust me and let me have time to win him more over. I will tell you everything as soon as I know it."

"My trust has been well earned by your family. So go, do whatever you must to find out about these witches." Athena touched a cold hand to the Athenians cheek and vanished. The trees fell back into place, and the forest felt as it did when he arrived. Zander rushed to fetch his horse and pushed down the whisper of guilt that teased at the edge of his heart. He knew his duty was to his goddess, but he couldn't hide from his betrayal of Nicos. Shaking it off and mounting his horse, he turned and galloped out of the cover of the forest to do as he had said he would to Nicos; find a place for the night.

***

The ride from the dianthus field to Iolkos took little over an hour. Thea asked Nicos many questions about his new companion, teasing him when his cheeks flushed scarlet when she inquired as to whether Nicos thought him handsome. Of course, she knew he did, even though all he offered in response were some half-garbled protestations. He told her too of how well Chiron had cared for him and that leaving the mountain had been as difficult as leaving the village. The village. They both stopped short; both horses lowered their heads to pull at the grass on the side of the road whilst their riders took a moment to gather themselves.

"Was it really as Artemis said?" Nicos' voice was soft, coated with sorrow.

"Mostly," Thea's voice trembled with a heart ache that threatened to break her. "I had just sent Korinna off to fetch something; I don't even remember now what it was, when

Artemis was at my side. I knew instantly something was wrong. We all did, I think.

"I saw him for the briefest of seconds, grey-haired, his face set in terrible anger. Then I was in the middle of the forest, the screams of the hunters, our family, echoed through the trees in some twisted cacophony. I made to run back, but Artemis held me fast. She held me so tight until the whole forest was silent. A mournful, sorrowful silence."

Nicos was close enough to reach out and take her hand. He squeezed it tightly as silent tears streaked down his face. Thea continued, lost in the horror of her memory.

"When her grip lessened, I tore from her and ran. As fast as Atalanta, if not quicker. The smell of burnt flesh and wood filled my nose before I even saw the village. When I did…" Thea trailed off, as she had no words to describe the devastation and horror that was left before her.

"I am so sorry." It seemed so feeble, but it was all Nicos could say.

Thea looked at him with watery, tired eyes.

"At least I have you still," she said with a weak smile. "Now come on, don't we need to find this handsome man of yours?"

"Enough mother," Nicos couldn't help but laugh a little. "He is not *my* handsome anything. Just a friend."

"Korinna and I were *just* friends at first too."

Thea gave a nudge for Zephyra to begin walking onwards, Nicos and Theron keeping perfect step beside them. In no time at all, they were passing through the streets of Iolkos. Most of the streets were empty by now, except for the last of the labourers making their way home or to a tavern. A rather inebriated man shouted some vulgar invitations, though whether it was to Thea or Nicos was unclear, as they turned down another street in search of Zander.

They pulled up and dismounted in the centre of the city, which during the day would be busy with stalls, now standing nearly empty under the gentle light of the crescent moon. Thea watched Nicos to see if he would use his gift of borrowed sight to find Zander and was surprised to see him doing something new. He had taken the ring forged in the hands of Aphrodite and Hephaestus and held it flat in his palm. Nicos closed his eyes and whispered some secret words of magic into the air. The gem-like vial on the ring pulsed with a rhythmic, soft red light. Thea watched in silence, afraid to speak in case it might interrupt whatever Nicos was doing.

Several minutes passed, and seemingly nothing was happening. Thea began to speak when she noticed the light of the ring was pulsing brighter and then brighter again. Nicos had opened his eyes, and a proud smile lit up his face. He folded his fingers over the ring and placed it back in his satchel.

"What did you do?" Thea asked.

"I called Zander to us," Nicos answered, unable to hide the satisfaction in his voice. He then pointed to a street across the way from them, just as a tall, broad Athenian came into view.

Nicos started to lead Theron towards Zander, with Thea following behind.

"Zander!" Nicos greeted warmly.

"My Nicos," Zander answered, his face looking a little bemused.

"Are you well?" Nicos asked, concerned.

Zander nodded. "Quite. Only I... You will think me mad, but I felt called to find you; only I knew exactly where to go."

Nicos grinned broadly.

"That would be the pull of a witch," Thea said, stepping up with her hand out stretched.

With a startled expression, Zander shook the hand proffered to him.

"Zander, this is Thea..."

"Your mother?" Zander interrupted. "I had no idea, hello. It's wonderful to meet you. I have heard much of the hunters. Through Nicos and reputation."

"A pleasure. I too have heard much of you," said Thea.

"Have you?" Zander's cheeks went pink.

"Have you got us a place to sleep tonight?" Nicos cut off a little sharper than he meant. He was desperate to stop any kind of suggestive talk of feelings that Thea and Zander threatened to begin. He didn't know how he felt about Zander, or rather, he didn't want to face his feelings yet. Zander nodded and led them for a few minutes through quiet streets to a house that had a small stable out front. There they left the horses, and taking their belongings from them, they followed him inside.

They sat at a table where a young man brought them a plate of bread and olives and set down a flask of sweet wine. Zander followed him off, saying he was going to sort out another room for Thea. With the exchange of some more drachmae, all was settled. The three ate whilst Thea conducted a gentle interrogation of Zander. She was hard-pressed to conceal her grin when the handsome Athenian spoke of Eros striking his heart and spoke so freely of his attraction as well as his intent towards Nicos. Nicos, during this, pretended he could hear nothing, keeping his eyes fixed on the olives, though he couldn't deny the warmth that spilled through him at Zander's words.

"It is time we all retire for the night, after all, tomorrow will be long, and it would be best we are rested," Thea said as she rose from the table. Zander and Nicos followed suit. Thea kissed Nicos on the cheek and held him close as she bid them goodnight, closing the door to her room behind her. Nicos followed Zander into their room to see that he had already carried all his things inside. He must have done it when sorting Thea's extra room, Nicos thought.

The room was quaint and small. A bed, a wooden bowl, and a bronze jug of water to wash themselves.

"I shall take the floor this time," Zander grinned as he poured the water into the bowl.

Nicos sat on the bed and pulled off his sandals. It was plenty big enough for two, he thought, and who knows when they would have a proper bed again, but he didn't want to send any wrong message. He resolved to say nothing for the moment and gratefully took the bowl of water from Zander and splashed some on his face before putting it on the floor by his feet.

"How was your meeting with…" Zander gestured towards the sky.

"It was… a lot." Nicos felt his weariness suddenly heavier. "Tomorrow we will ride to the port of Pagasae, where you and Thea need to find a friend by the name of Alyosha who has a boat for us."

"Where will you be?" Zander sat at Nicos' feet, facing him. He wet some cloth, and gently took Nicos' foot into his hand, and washed it clean.

A sigh of relief and something else escaped Nicos' mouth. "I have to meet with Poseidon."

Zander paused to look up at his friend.

"Yeah. I need to ask for him for something, and the others think it's best I do it face-to-face."

"Others?" asked Zander, now washing the other foot.

"Artemis, Apollo and…" Nicos trailed off.

"You can trust me you know." Zander stood to throw the water out the window, then returned the bowl to its place.

"I know. I do… it's just… I have something for you." Nicos pointed at his satchel. Zander picked it up and threw it to him. He caught it and pulled out the divinely made ring.

"It's beautiful!" Zander exclaimed as he took the ring from Nicos, turning it over in his hand. "I have never seen something so exquisitely made. It must have cost you a fortune, I couldn't accept such a gift."

"You can really. It's to keep you safe and hidden from anything with the gift of sight." Nicos stood now to face him and slipped the ring onto Zander's right finger between the middle and the little. "This here," he pointed to the crystal, "is my magic."

Zander wasn't looking at the ring now, just into the eyes of the man before him. "You made this for me?"

"With the help of some friends," Nicos met Zander's gaze. The air around them felt thick; it danced with electricity. Nicos pressed his lips to Zander's. His lips were soft and full, his beard bristled against his skin. He felt one of Zander's hands cradle his face; the other was at his back, pulling him closer. It took a great deal of strength for Nicos to finally break free from the kiss. His first kiss. He pushed himself away slightly and swallowed hard.

"Sorry," Nicos looked away, embarrassed.

"I'm not," Zander beamed.

Nicos gave a small laugh before turning his back on Zander, desperate to calm his racing heart. "We should get to sleep."

"We should." He could hear that Zander was still smiling even with his back turned.

They both undressed, and Nicos blew out the candles that lit the room before slipping under the bed cover. He watched as Zander pulled a blanket over himself on the floor.

"You can sleep up here with me if you want." Nicos tried to say in a nonchalant tone, though he was sure his voice quivered when he spoke. "There is room enough, I mean…"

"Are you sure?" Zander was already on his feet and sliding under the bed covers.

"Mmhmm." Nicos felt the warmth of Zander's bare skin as he lay on his back beside him.

"Relax, Nicos, nothing will happen between us unless you want it too," Zander said reassuringly.

Nicos let out the breath he had been holding. He knew that already, but hearing Zander say it aloud eased him.

"Thanks."

23

The port of Pagasae was a vibrant harbour. A plethora of ships of varying sizes were docked, some just returning, others ready to set sail. The blue of the sea was in sharp contrast to the white of the sails, most hoisted to the mast billowing slightly in the steady breeze whilst others were furled. A few ships displayed rich, colourful sails, denoting that they belonged to some wealthy merchant, and then amongst all these were the humble fishing boats unloading their first catch of the day. The air was filled with the smell of salt, fish, and spices. People were scurrying around, like busy worker ants, unloading ships of fabrics and spices, some were carried straight to stalls to be sold, with the rest being transported to nearby warehouses.

Nicos, Zander, and Thea arrived in the early morning. Helios was only just beginning his journey across the clear sky. It struck Nicos that Athens had been alive, but Pagasae held a different vibrancy of life. The citizens seemed happier, and perhaps there seemed to be a real order to the hustle and bustle in comparison to that of Athens.

The three stood facing the harbour, looking out to the calm ocean water that lay beyond the entrance to the port. He had never been on the wide ocean before. Now he was meant to leave mainland Greece and sail to far-off islands. Nicos' breath caught in his chest. Was this excitement, or fear, or both that he felt? Thea noticed his held breath, placed her hand on his back and rubbed it affectionately, much like she did when he was a child.

"What's the plan, then?" Zander asked as he watched a small fishing boat sail out of the mouth of the harbour.

"I want you both to find Alyosha and ready anything that may have been overlooked, food and the like, whilst I go and meet with Poseidon." Nicos sounded confident in his instructions, even though inside he felt nauseous.

Thea nodded and started off down the docks, hunting for the friend of Artemis. Zander hung back a moment and took Nicos' hand in his before whispering, "Are you sure you want to go alone?" He sounded concerned.

Nicos smiled at him and said, "I am sure, and even if I wasn't, I think it's the only way."

"Zander!" Thea called from the docks.

"See you soon, then." Zander kissed the knuckles on Nicos hand as he turned on his heel and ran to catch up with Thea, whose face was covered in a broad smile.

Nicos walked a little way into the port town, trying to locate a spot out of sight of everyone.

He ducked into a narrow-cobbled street so he could cast his eyes into one of the many gulls that circled the skies. He searched for a private place to summon the God of the Sea and quickly found a slim strip of beach, a cove of some sort.

There.

A mile or so away, a perfect small cove of jagged rocks nestled on a small strip of white sand.

It took no time at all to reach the cove, which sat a little way off a road leading towards the east of the town. The road was quiet and pleasant enough. A cool, light breeze caressed his face which seemed to help keep Nicos calm. The calmness increased as the familiar feeling of a spell began to tease him; it was a cloaking of some sort. Only it didn't feel as though it was one of his own workings, it felt familiar, but there was something else in it, like a secret hidden in his blood.

Most of his magic worked by him remembering images that told him what he needed, but this felt like the whisper of a female voice speaking some secret words to him. At first, he thought to distrust this magic, as though it may be planted by some evil enchantress, but the voice was warm, almost nurturing. So, as he had done with all his magic before, he let it swirl and form in his mind.

As Nicos left the path to walk down a grassy slope, he stopped and dropped behind a shrub. For all his years living with the hunters, he had mastered the feeling of knowing when something new and dangerous was nearby. It only took a second for him to hear the change in the animals around him and the hair on his neck stand on end. Cautiously, he glanced through the shrubs up the sloping hillside, and there at the top, he saw them. A group of women standing together at the hill's highest point. There was something wrong, Nicos thought. These women looked wild, and amongst them stood a blonde-haired man, a good foot taller than them. He had a glow about him.

It was a god. He wasn't yet sure which one, but something in his distant memory was fighting to reveal itself. Nicos watched from his hiding place as the women ran down the hillside at great speed, like uncaged beasts. As they reached the road, they took off towards Pagasae. The mysterious Olympian stood watching from his vantage point. Then he was gone in the blink of an eye.

Nicos' heart was hammering against his ribs as he launched to his feet, debating whether to run back towards Thea and Zander. No. It was no coincidence that these people, whoever they were, had shown up now in Pagasae. They had to be looking for him. A hunter always based their judgement on logic, not emotion. Thea would keep Zander and herself safe. No one knew about them, right? Also, if they had found Alyosha, then surely they would help to, if indeed they needed help. He had to go on. The sooner he summoned Poseidon, the sooner he could return to them. With one last look towards the port, he carefully climbed down over the jagged white rocks and dropped on to the small strip of sand inside the cove.

Looking around, he saw a shallow cave, the floor of which was covered in an inch or more of sea water. This was the perfect place to meet the brother of Zeus. As Nicos reached the cave entrance, he paused as the final piece of magic came into place. He took his dagger from his belt, pricked his finger, and let a single drop of blood stain the tip. He moved it from left to right in an arc marking the cave entrance over his head as the word *krymménos* fell from his lips, echoing gently. Nicos turned then to walk into the sea, just past his ankles, and spoke aloud into the air.

"Great Poseidon, King of the Sea, mighty earth shaker, I humbly implore you to grace me with your presence." The words felt uncomfortable in his mouth —this performative begging. He was about to recite the plea again when, rising up from the water just beyond the coves entrance, appeared the great God, Poseidon.

It seemed a truth of all Olympians that they could steal your breath with their beauty, as Nicos let out a gasp at the sight of Poseidon. He wore a gold crown that was decorated with gemstones of polished lapis lazuli and aventurine, the colours looking as though the sea itself were held atop his head.

As he came closer, Nicos noticed the rivulets of blues and greens tracing over his whole dark-skinned body like tiny rivers. He loomed in front of him now, his foam-green robe clinging to his body, and for a long time no one spoke. Nicos stared into the haunting ocean eyes of Poseidon, trying to mask any fear that threatened to break him, then purposefully he dropped to one knee, and bowed his head in reverence.

"So, this is the mortal who frightens my brother." Poseidon's voice was rough like waves breaking against a rocky shore.

"If you would come with me, great Poseidon, I have a place we may speak with no fear of being overheard or discovered," Nicos said.

He rose to his feet, leading the way into the cave. Poseidon was taken aback by the instruction but followed the flow of the water inside the cave. As he crossed through the cave's entrance, he felt as though the air had turned thick, like mud, and for a moment it burnt his skin.

"What was that?" he asked angrily.

"I protected this place with my magic, it can be uncomfortable for your kind at times," answered Nicos, taking some pride that his witchery caused some brief discomfort to the god before him.

Poseidon eyed him for a moment and before asking, "Why have you summoned me, Son of Circe?"

"I need your help." It was a simple statement, said honestly enough, but it sang like sweet music in Poseidon's ears. The god couldn't keep the arrogant grin from teasing up the corners of his mouth. He waved his hand for Nicos to continue.

"I need your aid in travelling across the seas." Nicos was annoyed at playing into the ritual of begging, his cheeks flushed slightly with embarrassment. "I have a ship, but no crew to row it, and there is fear winds may be tempered by Zeus. I thought that perhaps you, great God of the Sea, have some way to speed me over the waters of Greece."

Poseidon stroked his close-cut beard and made a noise, a low humming of thought.

"Why should I help you, boy?"

"Because…" Nicos began.

"Well?"

"For Greece. Don't do it to aid me; do it to save Greece and all her people," Nicos answered. A flicker of surprise danced across Poseidon's face.

"I am on a journey to gather things that will save Greece and aid in the war between you and the other Olympians," Nicos continued. "I don't know its purpose yet, but I know that I, with the help of those gods who stand against Zeus, will save Greece and the world from certain destruction." He had never said the full weight of his burden out loud before, and now, as he did so in front of the Sea God, he felt a rush of power. As well as a flash of humiliation at having to play the meek mortal to an arrogant god.

"What will you do for me in return?" asked Poseidon.

"Pardon?" said Nicos.

"Did I stutter mortal?" Poseidon rumbled.

"No…"

"Then answer my question!" he ordered.

Nicos looked the god square in the eye and summoned all his courage to keep him from shaking. He had come with humility, as Demeter had suggested, but still he was faced with the arrogance that ran through all of those who dwell on Olympus. He had to earn something from them and give more than he already had.

"Nothing," he said.

Poseidon looked furious at Nicos' response, just as he was about to chastise the young man. Nicos held up his hand to silence the god.

"Yesterday I met with the Olympians who stand against Zeus and his barberry, it was they who asked me to come meek and mild to seek your aid." Nicos voice was tense with controlled anger.

Poseidon looked at him with a cold expression.

"But I believe now they were wrong. You may be against Zeus, but you do not stand with us. You will not help me over the seas unless I do you some pointless task. Even though you know I am hunted by Zeus, Ares, Athena, Hera, Dionysius, and Hermes. Each one with their followers seeking to find and kill me and anyone who is with me. I am already risking my life because of the petulant, childish fear of one god; I will not waste my time with another!" Nicos turned and headed out of the cave.

"You will not cross these seas without me, boy!" Poseidon boomed.

Something in Nicos snapped, it was hard to say what, but with fierce eyes, he turned, raising a hand towards the cave he bellowed.

"SFARIGDA!"

The cave walls shook as they glowed for a moment of a second. Fear broke the fierceness of Poseidon's face. It was something to see a god afraid.

"What did you do, boy?" Poseidon asked, trying hard to sound unbothered.

"I am not a boy! My name is Nicos, the witch son of Circe, great witch of Aeaea." Nicos held a wildness in him that seemed to be pulled from the earth itself. "You could have helped me; helped all of Greece, but you, in your arrogance, couldn't do it. So, I have trapped you in this cave until my journey is done."

Poseidon let out a cold, heartless laugh and made to leave. As he was about to cross the entrance, that familiar thick air met him, only this time it was almost impenetrable. He pushed his palms hard against the invisible barrier. An agonised scream echoed around the cave as his skin began to burn. He recoiled and looked at his blistered hands. In a rage, Poseidon raised his hands, and below him, the sea water in the cave began to swell as great waves crashed against the invisible blockade.

Nicos could feel their force smashing into his spell, if it had been anything else, it surely would have shattered, but his magic held strong. Eventually the water subsided to reveal a livid Poseidon standing wet and wild, trapped in the witch's prison. He held out a hand in front of him, his face twisted in focus. Nicos looked over his shoulder to the sea. A feeble flurry of small waves hit the shore, but then the sea was calm once more.

"How?" Poseidon whispered.

"I am just like my mother!" Nicos said forcefully, "Now, shall we try this again? I will release you as long as you promise to help me... Please."

Poseidon gave a small nod.

Nicos was more himself again, the wildness that had overcome him had been tamed as he moved towards the trapped Poseidon, who watched him cautiously. "Will you help my boat to sail over the seas?"

"Yes," The Sea God's voice was softer than before. "I give you the waves, they are yours to command. Tell them where you wish to go, and they will carry you to your destination."

"Anoixe," Nicos whispered as he waved his fingers, and the cave glowed as it did before.

Poseidon disappeared in a sudden wave before Nicos could say another word. He watched the ocean become choppy and threatening. He would have to trust that Poseidon would be true to his word.

24

Zander caught up to Thea just as she turned down to the docks proper. The water under the boats was calm and clear, so clear you could see fish darting around under the surface. Zander made a polite apology for dawdling, as he put it, but Thea just grinned at him knowingly. The two meandered past fish sellers and men lumbering down gang planks carrying crates of goods from the merchant ships. Thea stopped suddenly as two children darted past giggling, one of them making a swipe for Zander's money pouch that hung at his hip, only to be stopped by Thea catching one of them by the wrist.

"You should be more careful," Thea said as she watched the young girl squirm in her grasp.

"Let go of my sister!" the young boy shouted.

"In a moment. Zander, give me two drachmae."

Zander hurried to pass over the money. His face held a puzzled expression, a similar look was on the face of the young boy that now stood by his side.

"I will release your sister and give you these coins if you can tell me where I might find a boat maker named Alyosha. Here, as a show of good faith." Thea released her grip on the young girl, who, rubbing her wrist, went to stand next to her brother. The sister and brother turned into each other and held a whispered council, occasionally, they threw up a suspicious glance towards the looming forms of Thea and Zander.

"Alyosha works down the south side of the port," said the young girl resolutely, brushing some of her unruly dark hair from her face. The boy snatched the coins from Thea's hand and the two darted off between the throng of people.

The south side of the port was much quieter in comparison. The shouting of those toing and froing faded to give way to the sound of chisels on wood and that of carpentry. This is where the ships were built and repaired. Only one ship stood finished amongst the towering skeleton frames of the others. It was a fantastic blue in colour, with golden eyes painted on either side of the bow. There was no doubt in either Thea or Zander's mind that this was the boat meant for them, as it was clearly built by the hands of gods, or, in the very least, by hands instructed by gods. Thea tapped Zander on the arm and pointed towards a hooded figure standing before the boat as still as a statue.

"Excuse me," asked Thea, "we are looking for Alyosha."

"Why?" A coarse voice replied from under the hood.

"We have been sent by a friend of the hunt," Zander said.

"Well, it's about time!" The figure lowered their hood to reveal a short, blonde-haired, androgenous beauty. Their face lit up when they smiled; without it, they looked fierce. The most striking thing about Alyosha, was their eyes, or rather the lack thereof. They must have had them once, but now they were just scarred flesh. "There are only two of you?"

"Yes…" Zander couldn't hide the curiosity in his voice.

"You learn to see differently when your eyes have been taken," Alyosha answered without hesitation or judgement. "Neither of you are Nicos?"

"No," said Thea, "I am his mother, not Circe…"

"Circe no, you are Thea of the hunters and indeed as much his mother as any."

Thea was touched by the kindness that oozed from Alyosha.

"I am Zander, son of Zenon, friend of Nicos," Zander held his hand forward.

"I was never told of you," they said simply. Zander retracted his hand. "Still, if you are here, then I am sure you are to be trusted. When will the Son of Circe be with us?"

Thea was about to answer when Alyosha suddenly held up their hand to silence her, their head tilted as though listening to something far away. In the distance, a scream carried along the wind —a word, though it wasn't clear what. The hunter's instinct took over Thea, and within the blink of an eye, she had her bow over her shoulder and an arrow from its quiver locked into place. Zander, following suit, had his hand at his sword, ready to unsheathe it.

"What is it?" he whispered.

"Something is happening on the other side of the harbour," answered Thea.

The scream had now become shouts of panic. From where they stood, Thea and Zander watched the people of Pagasae run in all different directions. A single word being shouted again and again.

"What are they saying?" asked Zander.

"Maenads!" Alyosha answered. "Follow me; they must not find you."

They darted into a warehouse full of wood and stone. Thea and Zander followed. Alyosha pointed for them to hide behind a large pile of timber that had been freshly sawn and sanded. The pair crouched behind the timber before they were covered with a grubby old sheet, hiding them from view.

"Whatever happens, do not reveal yourselves," Alyosha whispered. "You must make it out of the port, or all and everything is lost."

It wasn't clear how long they stayed crouched behind the pile of wood, but the shouts and screams didn't seem to die down for a long time. When it did, however, an eerie silence fell over the town, with only the soft lapping of the waves outside providing any sound at all.

"Should we..." Zander was cut off by Thea clamping a hand over his mouth. His brow furrowed, but then he heard it.

"In there!" came a wild voice from outside. Five or so maenads stalked into the warehouse, they hummed a strange tune as they searched. Thea and Zander were barely breathing. They watched the shadows of the hunting followers of Dionysus through the sheet that covered them, hearts in their throats. Just as one of them reached out a dirty, long-nailed hand to pull back the fabric, Alyosha's voice sounded from somewhere unseen to them.

"There is no one here, mad women of Dionysus."

The maenads turned on their heels and deftly, like a pack of lionesses, encircled them. The women were dressed in torn, flowing dresses made of a near-see-through material the colour of rich red wine. Each one had ivy woven through wild hair and eyes that held the same wide pupil, making them seem black and hollow. The tallest of them straightened herself up a little and looked Alyosha in the face.

"Who said we were looking for someone?" Her voice was raspy and dangerous.

"To whom am I speaking?" Alyosha asked calmly.

"I am Dyna, devotee to the great God, Dionysus, and leader of his maenads." Dyna gave an extravagant bow. "To whom do I speak?"

"Alyosha of Pagasae, ship builder." They could feel the women tightening their circle around them. "I am no threat to you or your women, I only wish to protect my home."

Dyna stalked forward, sniffing at Alyosha, like a dog catching the scent of something to memorise. She stood less than an inch from their face. Alyosha could smell the wine on her breath, making their nose wrinkle. It might have been a relief for them to be blind in this moment, as they couldn't see the frightening smile that Dyna wore, showing that her teeth were filed into sharp points.

"You are strong, you should join us." Dyna's voice was just above a whisper, and from all around, the other maenads started to chant in discordant harmony. Alyosha felt as though their head were swimming, as if they had drunk too much wine. The women around them moved in closer and swayed with arms on each other's shoulders whilst Dyna put her palm on Alyosha's forehead. They felt their mind getting foggier under the need to surrender to the will of the maenads.

"Welcome my…" Dyna stopped at the sound of a cry coming from the other side of the port. She and the other maenads tore from the warehouse in the direction of the sound. Alyosha fell to their knees as their mind restored itself.

Thea crept cautiously from their hiding place and moved to the door to see where the wild women had gone. Zander, who had followed just behind, put an arm around Alyosha.

"Are you alright?" he asked.

"I feel as though I just woke up from a drunken stupor," Alyosha said as Zander helped them to their feet.

"What distracted them?" Thea sounded worried. "You don't think…?"

* * *

Nicos stood watching the sea froth and foam, unable to ignore the guilt that had settled in his stomach. It was never his intention to anger the mighty Sea God, but the audacity of him to be asked a *favour.* Was facing down Zeus and saving Greece not enough? The magic that he used to bind the god in the cave was his, but it felt different somehow. His witchery had always flowed in the same pattern, everything falling into place exactly as he needed it and as he understood it, learning and memorising each step so it would become second nature. But this magic came from deep within the very fabric of his being —wild and untamed. He barely held onto himself. He thought then of the haunting female voice that had echoed in his mind before he had met with Poseidon. Nicos had heard the voice before, but when and where?

Nicos had been so lost in thought that he hadn't noticed he had begun walking back towards Pagasae. It was only when he stumbled on a loose rock that he realised he was back on the road. He shook his head, trying to clear the fog of confusion so he could focus on the task at hand.

Hopefully Thea and Zander have had an easier time finding Alyosha, he thought.

As he passed the spot he had hidden behind, Nicos remembered with sharp clarity the women he had watched cascade down the mountain and the Olympian that stood amongst them. It was like a cold drop of water landing at the base of his neck as he remembered in which direction they had been running. Towards the harbour. Towards Thea and Zander.

His feet started running before he knew it, his heart hammering in his chest. He ran as fast as Nike, if not faster, nothing and no one could keep pace with him. In the years he was raised by the hunters, he had mastered the art of running without making a sound. Nicos slipped like a shadow into the harbour walls and ducked behind a pile of fishing nets, narrowly avoiding being knocked into by panicked citizens.

"GET INSIDE!" a panicked mother shouted, shepherding a group of crying children through an open door and slamming it behind her.

A wild-haired woman threw herself at the closed door, banging her fists on it and screaming incoherently. Nicos unsheathed his kopis and went to grab the crazed woman, but stopped short as three more of them ran past, sweeping up the other with them.

He needed to get a better view of the port but couldn't risk sharing eyes with a bird, as it would leave him too vulnerable. He had to get up higher. Silently, he slipped from behind the fish nets and made his way to the side of the house where the mother was hiding with the children. He creeped past a window with its shutters closed, but through a crack in the painted blue wood, he saw a group of children huddled together. The woman he had heard shouting came into view and caught him looking through.

"Pssst…" Nicos whispered, casting his eyes around to make sure none of the mad women were nearby. "Can you tell me, who are these people?"

The woman crossed over to the window. "They are the followers of Dionysus," she said in a quiet, timid voice.

"Maenads?!" Nicos was shocked.

Maenads weren't known to be in this area of Greece, not in such great numbers at least. The little he knew of them was that they kept to themselves, and only when their private blood worship of Dionysus was disturbed did they become murderous. There had been stories, too, that when they moved through towns to recruit new followers, if anyone got in their way, then they would tear them limb from limb. It would be a huge coincidence if what was going on now was just recruitment gone wrong. Then another thought came to him, one that made him more nervous than he wanted to admit. The Olympian he had seen, the one who had been so close, was the God of Wine himself, Dionysus. How did they know he was here?

"Do you know why they're here?" Nicos asked.

"They are looking for someone."

Nicos had known the answer before she said it.

"I am going to distract the maenads, and when you can, run! I want you to take the children and run." With that said, Nicos climbed up the side of the house. All the years of climbing trees back with the hunters made scaling the wall easy enough. He pulled himself up on to the flat roof, and being careful not to let anyone see him, he took in the view of the once-organised chaos of the docks that was now filled with people running, hiding, and fighting.

The majority of the wild women of Dionysus seemed to be searching the western side, where it looked like most of the living quarters seemed to be, to the south, he could see a shipbuilders' yard and warehouses. Nicos noted a group of five maenads were skulking towards one of the warehouse buildings; it wouldn't mean anything if he hadn't caught sight of a hooded figure seemingly stalking them. Nicos knew he needed a closer look. He cast his sight into a rat that was scuttling on the street below and urged it towards the stalker of the maenads.

The rat moved quickly over ropes and boxes, narrowly avoiding being trampled on by some of the still-fleeing harbour folk. By the time the rat reached the warehouse, the maenads had surrounded the now-hoodless stalker, who announced themselves as Alyosha. The rat squeaked in alarm, though no one paid it any mind.

Nicos' eyes were his own again, his brain whirring to come up with a plan to distract the maenads, to help Alyosha and the inhabitants of Pagasae. The majority of the followers were still searching the westside and amongst the ships. If he could just get those in the warehouse over to the west, it would give time for the children in the house below to run and for him to get to Alyosha. Carefully, he jumped down from the roof and landed like a cat on the stone road. He moved then and wrapped his knuckles on the still-closed shutters of the window.

"Be ready," Nicos said firmly.

He ran to the cover of the fishing nets he had previously hidden behind. There, he sat on the ground. Then, as he had done with a handful of snakes once before on Mount Pelion, Nicos cast his mind into every rat that lived within the harbour. The ground began squirming, shifting as hundreds upon hundreds of brown rats poured from every crack and corner of the place.

They charged towards the maenads, driving them towards the west entrance of Pagasae. Many of them lashed out, grabbing at the rodent army. Some of the women snatched up a rodent and tore it in half, sending blood splattering everywhere. They laughed coldly, relishing the feeling of the warm blood that now painted their faces.

Nicos felt sick.

In retaliation, he had the rats swarm up the maenads, forcing them to the ground as they bit and clawed at them in vengeance. A deadly cry called out from the dying women, it was echoed by her sister followers. Still, the rats kept swarming, drowning them in their furry bodies, except for those that had fallen beyond the western entrance, they were left unharmed.

The quick padding of bare feet thudded past Nicos in his hiding place, informing him that the wild women in the warehouse were heading towards their distressed sisters. He wouldn't have long once he broke his connection with the rats. He had to time this right. Nicos watched through the eyes of the rodents as the new maenads reached them. They looked wilder and more ferocious than any he had seen yet. He could hear the bone-chilling primal scream that tore from the woman who had been face-to-face with Alyosha. With one last push, Nicos urged the rats to attack those maenads that still stood within the walls of Pagasae, and then he broke the connection, sprinting towards the warehouse.

25

"I think we need to get on the boat and..." Alyosha was cut off again by Thea.

"Respectfully, Alyosha, we need to get out of Pagasae to find Nicos!" Her voice was tight with emotion. She couldn't bear to lose anyone else. Thea had her bow and arrow in her hand, ready to make her run for it, when Zander caught her by the arm. She was about to protest when she looked at where he was pointing. There in the doorway stood Nicos.

They both were on him in no time, pulling him into a crushing three-way embrace. Alyosha stood patiently to the side, keeping their focus fixed in the direction of where the group that had surrounded them had fled.

"I'm fine," Nicos said, "We don't have a lot of time. The boat?"

"It's ready if you have a way to move it?" Alyosha answered calmly.

"I do. We need to move before..." Nicos didn't get to finish that sentence.

The whole of Pagasae had become deathly silent. Nicos turned on his heel as he drew his sword. Thea was at his right shoulder, bow still in hand, and Zander was on his left with his own sword drawn. Alyosha, too, had come up to stand next to Thea, two curved blades in hand that they had unsheathed from their back. Nicos could see that the rats had now dispersed back to their hiding places, and the maenads that still stood, much fewer in number, made their way back into the town. They climbed over the bodies of their fallen sisters, through the spilled blood of rats and humans.

"What is it, Nicos?" Zander asked, noticing his face had gone pale. "What do you see?"

There, moving amongst the maenads, looking incredibly out of place, was the golden, curly haired form of...

"Dionysus."

Nicos felt the three Grecians beside him tense.

"We need to get you out of here now," Thea said, fighting hard to sound calm.

Alyosha grabbed Nicos by the wrist and started dragging him towards the beautiful blue ship that bobbed gently in the water. Silently, they climbed the gang plank, Nicos moving quickly to make sure to keep his eyes on Dionysus. Thea and Zander began to raise the anchor whilst Alyosha pulled the gang plank up on the ship.

"Nicos," the warm, sweet sound of Dionysus filled the air. "Son of Circe don't be afraid, little witch. Come and face the God of Wine! You killed my women easy enough, will you not face down a god with your power?" A sickly-sweet laugh echoed around the harbour.

"We are ready to go." Alyosha whispered, their eyeless face fixed in the direction that Dionysus stood. Nicos seemed unable to move.

"We can't," Nicos said quietly. "If he sees the ship, then no port in Greece will be safe."

He watched the reality dawn on all of their faces.

"Come now, little witch," Dionysus spoke again, "do you hide like your rats?" This time, his words were coated in venom. It surprised Nicos that he seemed to truly care for his fallen wild women.

"How do we stop him from seeing us?" Zander asked.

It was like a spark went off in Nicos' mind. The idea came like a spell, only it was more sudden and much fiercer. Instead of pulling from his witchery, he knew he needed to pull from the divinity that flowed through him. He took Thea's bow from her hand and quickly pulled two arrows from the quiver at her back. She looked at him, puzzled, but before she could question his actions, Nicos was leaping from the boat and running towards the skeleton frame of another ship, a short way from them.

Zander and Thea watched with mouths agape as Nicos put the arrows between his teeth, flung the bow over his shoulder, and began to clamber up the ship's frame. They watched as he pulled himself up one beam to then jump on to another, climbing as nimbly as a cat, his feet never missing their mark. Soon he was shimmying his way up the mast that stood tall without sails. He pulled himself up to stand on the very top.

The wind, though still no more than a gentle breeze, felt stronger up here. Nicos had kept his balance in tougher situations than this. Carefully, he notched one of the arrows into place and took aim. If he missed, then this could mean the end of everything. Taking a steady breath, Nicos pulled back the arrow. He knew that a normal mortal-made arrow would have no effect, but if he could just channel Apollo's light into the tip, then maybe… hopefully…

Nicos closed his eyes to focus on the light of Apollo. That light he had tapped into on Mount Pelion. He breathed deeply into the need to protect his mother, his friend, and Alyosha. He thought about the woman who was hiding with all those children.

A gentle, sizzling sound caught in his ear.

Opening his eyes, Nicos saw the arrowhead was covered in a bright, dazzling light.

"Dionysus!" Nicos bellowed.

The God of Wine and Insanity looked up to see Nicos. A wicked, cruel smile danced across his face. He had the same hollowed-out black eyes as his maenads.

"You are a pretty little thing, aren't you!" Dionysus spoke like a lecherous drunk. "Come down here to me, child, so I can rip you limb from limb." His maenads howled in excitement. It was fascinating to Nicos how quickly the Olympian's tone had changed each time he spoke.

The first arrow left the bow with a twang, and a second later, the second one followed. Nicos watched them race through the air towards their target, the light burning brighter as they flew faster. For a moment, it felt like time had slowed. Nicos saw the sick grin on Dionysus' face as he too watched in amusement, the mortal-made arrows getting ever closer. It was clear, he thought, they would do him no harm.

How wrong he was!

The first arrow pierced his right eye, and a fraction of a second later, the second arrow lodged into his left. The scream that erupted from the god was like nothing the world had ever heard before. It shook the earth and burnt in the ears of those nearby. Time regained its normal speed as the maenads swarmed around their god. Nicos had to move, he slid down the mast and ran as fast as he could back towards the blue ship.

Thea saw him running. She realised the gang plank had been pulled up.

"Quick, we need to…" Thea shouted, but stopped when she saw Alyosha had already thrown a rope over the side and Nicos was pulling himself up. Zander was there, ready to help pull Nicos over the wooden railing.

"How did you…? What did you just do?" Zander asked as Nicos let go of his hand and ran to the bow of the ship. Alyosha, Thea, and Zander stood together, watching as Nicos called out to the sea.

"Take us to sea now! Poseidon, if you hear me, now is the time to pick a side. We need you… I need you to help us leave unseen… Please!!!" Nicos made no effort to hide his desperation.

With a great lurch, the boat began to move. It turned itself towards the mouth of the harbour and began sailing towards the wide ocean beyond. Zander ran up to stand by Nicos to look out over the edge to see how they were moving, but just as he reached him, two terrifying things happened at once.

A crack of white lightning struck next to the spot where Dionysus had now dropped to his knees. The arrows had been pulled from his eyes, but they were still wounded, each socket oozing thick golden ichor. As the lightning hit the ground, a great wall of sea water shot up along the whole length of the harbour; it must have been nearly a hundred feet tall. Thea gasped and then proceeded to describe what was happening to Alyosha. Zander grabbed Nicos' hand in his, holding it tightly.

The ship gained speed. As it broke the mouth of the harbour, the once-clear sky started to disappear in a growing sea fog. Poseidon, it seemed, had finally made his choice.

Nicos ran towards the stern of the ship, dragging Zander with him as he watched the wall of water still standing. The sea fog was clouding their view, but not before they all watched unrelenting bolts of lightning strike again and again all over the harbour of Pagasae. As they were fully lost into the fog, thunder rumbled loudly overhead.

26

The once-great harbour of Pagasae was now a smoking pile of rubble. No building was left standing, and all the boats had been sunk. The ground was littered with the burnt bodies of men, women, and children and there, standing amongst them, facing out into the fog beyond the harbour wall, was Zeus. His face held all the fury of the sky above, dark, and thunderous, and his fingers crackled with electricity. Beside him, whimpering on the floor, was Dionysus in a pool of golden ichor, with the handful of maenads that had been spared tending to him.

"Father," Athena had appeared along with Hera, Hermes, and Ares, "what happened here?"

Zeus said nothing.

"Dionysus?" Hera went over to the Wine God to help him to his feet, each of his devotees fell back on their knees, prostrating themselves on the floor. When Hera caught sight of his face properly, she gasped. His eyes of violet had healed, but two scarred lines ran vertically over his eyelids, permanently marking his injury.

"I almost had him!" Dionysus spat. "That little bastard witch! Then he shot two cursed arrows, blinding me." He put his fingers to his eyes and whimpered as he felt the unhealing scars. "He has disfigured me."

None of the gods present could deny the swell of unease that passed amongst them all. Never had anything other than a god been able to harm them; even then, they could make a full recovery. This witch had been able to blind and scar an Olympian, it was the first taste of the power they stood against. A thought did occur to Athena that if the Son of Circe was so powerful, why hadn't he just killed Dionysus?

Zeus still said nothing. He just stood, glaring out at the ocean.

"Did Nicos do this too?" Ares asked, looking around at the destruction.

No one answered, but Dionysus looked over at his father. Ares understood.

Athena had begun moving amongst the debris, her mind working out how one man had bested a whole group of wild maenads, as well as her divine brother. She picked up the arrows that had been pulled from the eyes of her brother to examine them. The light of Apollo still coated their end, gingerly, she touched it and felt a sharp scratch.

"The child has gifts of Apollo," Athena announced, although it was more like she was working things out aloud. "The arrows are mortal but coated in his divine light. It's got something else in it—a touch of witchcraft, no doubt—but this is how he can harm us. Where did he shoot from?"

Zeus cast a glance over his shoulder in her direction as Dionysus pointed to a mast that stood smoking amongst its smouldering ship frame.

"Incredible aim from such a distance," Athena continued. "Skilled with a bow, might I say, again, divinely so. Artemis has her hand in this too, somehow. Tell me, how did he know you were here?"

Zeus turned to face Dionysus now. Hera and Ares stood side by side, each watching Athena as her grey eyes scanned the bodies of maenads and rats littering the floor.

"Well," Dionysus began, "my wild women stormed the harbour, and then the rats began to kill them. I came and called for him to face me!"

"You declared your arrival?" Athena's said cooly.

"I just did as father instructed!" Dionysus shouted.

Zeus had his hand around the young gods throat in an instant. "I told you to capture him and summon me so I could kill him!" Zeus roared, choking his son.

"Husband, enough!" Hera commanded, placing her thin hand on Zeus shoulder. "Now is not the time to lessen our ranks."

Zeus dropped his son into the pool of his ichor once more.

"I want that witch found and killed," Zeus' eyes danced with lightning.

"Why not send a storm out over the seas," Ares suggested.

"Idiot!" Zeus lashed out, back-handing Ares across the face. "Do you think I am as simple-minded as you? My dear brother has taken his side, I cannot attack, nor can any of us, whilst they are in his domain. The ancient creed of Olympus forbids it."

"Father, I didn't mean to suggest…" Ares sounded like a beaten dog, his red eyes stung with an unexpressed rage.

"What do we do now?" Zeus turned to Athena.

Athena thought for a moment. "Well, my spy is close by his side, we can rely on him to keep sharing information. On our next meeting, I shall ask him to describe the ship so we can put watchmen and allies in every port of Greece. Until then, I think it is wise to prepare every follower at our disposal to spread the word of a dangerous male witch. One that levelled the town of Pagasae without cause."

Hera smirked at the cunningness of Athena's plan. Ares looked disgruntled, he craved battle and bloodshed.

"By spreading this tale, it will put every Grecian on alert," Athena continued. "It would be best if we could round up the Olympian traitors to stop them from giving any aid. We should be searching for them as much as him."

"We cannot find them," Hera said. "They have been cloaked from us, like the witch."

"So, we go to their places of favour. Draw them out," Athena said plainly.

"Do it." Zeus commanded.

"There will be no going back from this husband." Hera said this before she and Ares vanished.

Dionysus gathered his few remaining maenads and mumbled an apology towards his father before turning into the air. Athena still remained.

"Father, may I speak freely?"

Zeus gave a nod.

"We are lucky, this time we can blame your destruction on Nicos, but you have to be more careful," Athena said gently.

Zeus grunted in response, "Is there anything else you can tell me?"

"Nothing more, father," Athena answered, before she too turned into the air, leaving Zeus alone amongst the ruins of Pagasae.

27

It was unclear to any of them on board how far they had made it out to sea before the boat came to a steady standstill. The fog that had surrounded them for what felt like hours now gave way to a bright, clean sky dotted with soft white clouds. Nicos' sharp hazel eyes searched the horizon in every direction, looking for any sign of land, but all he could see was flat, dark blue water. Letting out a sigh of relief, he dropped onto the deck, his body releasing all the tension that it had been holding long before they arrived at Pagasae.

He could feel Thea's eyes on him as she busied herself talking with Zander. They were looking at a map of some kind, trying to figure out where they might be. Zander suggested they wait until nightfall to be sure of their position, as they would be able to use the stars as their guide. Nicos was grateful for the reprieve from the concern.

All through the fog he had recounted his meeting with Poseidon and of the mysterious voice that had whispered in his head, feeding him words of power and how he had bound Poseidon in the cave with the words that came from this unknown place. Thea had said nothing, whilst Zander looked at him as though only now was he realising just how dangerous he might be. It occurred to Nicos that this was the first time Zander had gotten a glimpse of his power, before this he had chosen to keep that hidden.

Nicos told them how he blinded Dionysus with light-tipped arrows. When asked by Zander how he could do that and aim so far, he told him the truth. Apollo and Artemis had given their blood to his mother to aid in his coming into being, so he had inherited gifts from them both. It seemed futile to hide anything from Zander now, even though there was still a niggling feeling that he should keep some of it secret. After that, there wasn't much left to say.

"I suppose now I can formally introduce myself," Alyosha said as they sat down next to Nicos.

Nicos smiled, "Hello."

"Are you alright?" Alyosha asked. It was a simple, honest question that caught Nicos completely by surprise.

"I don't know." Nicos turned to face Alyosha, he hadn't noticed their scarred, eyeless face properly. "Today it felt…" he paused, searching for the right word, but it wouldn't come.

"It is overwhelming to put into practice what you have spent time talking about," Alyosha said with wisdom that seemed beyond their years.

Nicos nodded, it was overwhelming. The magic was his but yet it felt strange in his body, then the use of Apollo's light, was new too. Chiron had prepared him for so much, yet now he felt as though he had learnt nothing at all and was starting again from the beginning. Nicos buried his face in his hands, and took some deep breaths, tasting the salt of the sea on his tongue. A strong arm wrapped itself around him. Looking up from his hands he was staring into the handsome face of Zander. He smiled at him before gently placing a kiss on his forehead. They stayed like this, not speaking for some time.

Nicos must have fallen asleep, as the next time he looked up, the sky was dark and littered with stars. He kissed Zander on the cheek as he slipped out from under his arm so as not to wake him, and he looked up to the dazzling night. It reminded him of being high up on Mount Pelion, stargazing with Chiron.

He spotted Ursa Major, his favourite of all the constellations. Nicos had always felt a connection to the great bear, a hapless victim of the gods' lust and jealousy. The legend, as he recalled it, was a young devotee of Artemis named Kallisto had become the lustful obsession of Zeus. The King of Olympus had tricked her by taking the form of the goddess she worshipped and to whom she had sworn her chastity.

Disguised as Artemis, he lured her away into a forest, where he pounced on her, had his way, and then left her broken on the ground. Months later, she gave birth to a son whom she named Arcas, who would go on to be King of Arcadia. The ending of the story was Kallisto being punished by being turned into a bear, though people differed in which god carried out her punishment. Some say it was Hera, enraged by her husband's infidelity; others say it was Artemis in fury at Kallisto breaking her vow of chastity. Whoever it was, Nicos always felt sorry for Kallisto. It seemed so unfair, yet so common, that she had to suffer for the actions of another.

Still, as a bear, Kallisto wandered the wild hills of Greece, escaping hunters for fifteen years, until one day a young man amongst a hunting party launched a spear that was sure to kill her. As the spear pierced through the bear's hide, Kallisto returned to her human form, and, in an instant, Artemis was by her side. Arcas was beside himself with shock, for it had been her son who threw the spear.

None of the gathered hunting party could believe their eyes, seeing the dying woman who had, moments before, inhabited the body of a bear, lying on the ground. Whether out of guilt or grief, Artemis summoned Zeus, begging him to raise Kallisto into the stars to live forever. He obliged, and so Kallisto became Ursa Major, the bear mother of the Arcadians.

Nicos had been so lost in remembering the story that he hadn't noticed Zander wake up.

"Beautiful," Zander said softly, looking at Nicos.

"It is, isn't it?" Nicos said whilst still looking at the stars. "Are you still glad you came to find me?"

"Of course." Zander turned Nicos to face him. "Why? Are you not?"

Nicos laughed, "Actually, I am. When I set out from my home, I thought I would be facing this all alone. I didn't mind. Even when we met again at Merope's I didn't think I needed or wanted anyone to come with me."

Zander frowned a little.

"She convinced me, you know?" Nicos carried on. "Merope. She said I wouldn't regret having you with me. She was right. Having you here, Thea, and Alyosha too, helps me remember what I am fighting for. I think it's all only going to get harder and more dangerous from here on out."

"I think you're right," said Zander, taking Nicos' hands in his. "We are all with you."

"I know. Can you fetch Thea and Alyosha for me?"

Zander gave his hand a squeeze, then went to find them. Nicos took some calming breaths and listened to the sounds of the ocean at night. It was peaceful, with water lapping at the still ship. He then thought of Poseidon and moved to the railing.

"Poseidon, thank you." Nicos spoke to the salt water below, he could swear he saw the face of the Sea God flash in the water. He turned around when he heard the soft footfall of Zander, followed by Thea and Alyosha.

"I'm sorry to wake you," Nicos said calmly, "I just thought you should all know where we are headed. I don't know what we will face or how difficult all that is to come will be, but before we go any further, I need to know if you wish to turn back."

Thea looked him straight in the eye and said, "Not a chance!"

"Never," Zander said with a conviction that made Nicos' heart leap.

"What, and miss the adventure to come?" Alyosha said with a wry smile.

Nicos couldn't help but return a smile. Once, he had thought this journey would be lonely, but now he had one of the greatest hunters of Artemis, a great man of Athens, and a blind shipbuilder. To call Alyosha a mere shipbuilder felt inadequate. Nicos knew there was more to them than that, and he looked forward to finding out all that that might be.

"Ok then," he said, "as soon as the sun breaks the horizon, we will be heading to the island of Ogygia."

"What's there?" asked Zander.

"Calypso."